Home for the Howliday

Cassie Leigh

This book is dedicated to three of the most amazing friends any girl could ask for: Barbara Malmberg, Mary Beth Willems, and Amanda Vavra. Your friendship has been unwavering and your belief in me humbling. I doubt I can ever thank you enough, but this is a start.

Acknowledgments

When I wrote this book, it came out fast and furious and I owe a lot to my editors Barbara Malmberg and Charlotte Penn Clark, as well as my publisher Dylan Moonfire with Broken Typewriter Press for helping me along the way. I also would like to say thank you to the Noble Pen writing group. They read the early chapters of this book and their advice helped it to take shape.

Home for the Howliday was a joy and a relief to write. It expresses a lighter side of myself that was itching to come out and combines my two greatest passions: shifters and MMA. I am obsessed with Mixed Martial Arts. It plays a small part in this book but you can expect more of it in this fictional world as I continue to write. While some find the sport brutal, I find it beautiful. I hope you love or at least appreciate it as much as I do!

Chapter 1

The sultry croon of "Santa Baby" blaring through the crowded cabin might as well have been nails on a chalkboard to Gunner Thoren. The eggnog and holiday cookie smorgasbord only added to his irritation. For the hundredth time he questioned his motivation for coming back into the fold. He'd walked away from a good thing in Las Vegas, to return home to the wolf-pack town of Ushers Run, Iowa. *"Eventually you all come home."* Gunner shook the pack-elder's voice from his already crowded mind. He'd met with the old man along with the pack-leader, Ambrose. It was a lofty position for his best friend to ascend to in Gunner's absence. Then Ambrose blindsided him with a compulsory invitation to attend the festivities this evening. It was intended for the younger members. Some crap about pack bonding.

Gunner just wanted to enjoy being in nature. It was the only part of being home that he looked forward to after a decade of self-imposed exile. The bright lights of Las Vegas lacked a forest for his wolf to run in. Wolves didn't belong skulking through back alleys and desert landscapes. At least Ambrose picked a nice spot in the woods for the cabin he'd designed for the pack's use. Too bad it was currently being overrun with someone's bastardized idea of Christmas cheer.

From his spot in the corner, Gunner sneered at the garish holiday sweaters covered in ice skating reindeer and penguins decorating evergreen trees. The pack he was born to, or at least this generation of it, might be happy to prance around like drunken fools, but he wouldn't be caught dead participating in such stupidity. His brother, Asher, loped toward him from across the room in the easy way that came with overstimulated youth. Battery-powered twinkle lights wrapped around the kid's snowflake-covered sweater. It must have come out of their grandmother's closet.

Asher grinned up at him. "You aren't in party gear, bro!"

Gunner growled and hunkered down in his corner, unwilling to acknowledge the fool. This kid was why he gave up fighting and the title shot he had worked for years to achieve. Now he would run his family's business—the local gym. With their father's passing, his mother needed the help keeping it from going under and his kid brother from tearing down half the town with his idiocy. Less than two years until he graduated and Gunner could take off again. He was already counting down the days.

"Never fear," Asher said, undaunted by Gunner's stoicism. "I knew it would happen, so I brought an extra."

Asher slapped his brother's back and gave him an ineffective shove that left the kid rubbing the sting out of his hand. Gunner stood still as a mountain, which he was as a middleweight fighter. He fought at 185 pounds but walked around closer to 220 between fights.

"Nothing's wrong with my sweater," Gunner groused. He'd worn a normal sweater, a traditional Scandinavian pattern in grey and navy. A respectable sweater, not some castoff thrift store reject.

"You're not getting into the spirit," Asher said, his tone sullen and accusatory.

Feminine laughter that was equal parts wicked and ethereal rose above the chaotic jumble of voices and crappy Christmas pop-music. Gunner tuned out the useless prattle that continued to dump out of his brother's mouth, searching for the owner of that laugh as if it was a homing beacon meant to draw him in.

"You've got enough for both of us." Gunner answered his brother to stop the distracting noise. He searched the nameless faces. The laughter had stopped but he knew he hadn't imagined its siren song.

That's when Gunner saw her. The reason he left town in the first place—Noelle Hiver. She moved like a Nordic goddess come to life—a young and beautiful version of the Norns—as she stood in front of a tinsel-draped tree talking with her hands as if they were weaving a tapestry to illustrate her words. The multicolored lights that reflected off the metallic decorations shone on her like a rainbow spotlight.

The little vixen was a dangerous temptation. Her white sweater dress embroidered with silver poinsettias hugged her lithe curves in places he knew his eyes shouldn't linger—but he couldn't stop himself, just like before. No one should look at the pack-leader's half-sister that way, not if he wanted to keep his eyes. His illicit gaze continued the treacherous journey north to wild platinum blonde hair that skimmed her slender shoulders. He wanted a closer look, perilous as it was. He needed to know if she still wore feathers braided in the riotous curls.

Noelle again laughed at something her companion said, a woman who didn't exist as far as Gunner was concerned, and it rang like bells calling him home. She glanced his way and his heart nearly stopped. Those eyes, guarded aquamarine glaciers, bored into him from across the room and he was curious what the pack abomination had made of herself.

He'd never called her that, but nearly everyone they knew had. A half-breed shifter witch was not welcome among purebred werewolves, but her brother Ambrose, Gunner's best friend, had changed that when he took over, hadn't he? At least for this one pack he had. Gunner had never worried about any of that as she was just Noelle to him.

He closed his eyes against visions of the past that clawed to the surface of his mind and realized his brother was still talking. "Bro, hotties heading our way. It's too late to fix you now." This time when Asher shoved, Gunner moved as his eyes flew open. Just a step closer to her but it was as if he jumped a chasm.

Noelle sauntered toward him, her friend in tow. A sweet smile spread across her pouty pink lips. A knowing smile. Gunner steeled himself against its impact. He knew this would come when he made the choice to return home. He just wasn't ready to see her tonight or for her to see him. But those lips brought a flash he'd give anything to forget, just to relieve the torture.

An image of her broke through, unbidden, from the past. That same smile as she sat waiting for him in the passenger seat of his Camaro on another winter night, reaching for something other than the gear shift, or at least not the one that belonged in his car.

"Gunner, fancy seeing you here." Noelle's silken voice pulled him out of the past.

"You're brother's invite clearly stated that I didn't have a choice."

Noelle smiled at the growl in his voice, clearly finding some kind of perverse pleasure in his words.

Asher glanced from Gunner to Noelle. "Dude, you know her?"

He's back. Noelle felt the heat of his gaze before she saw him, but once she did her feet were compelled toward him. It was as if Gunner was north and her inner compass had no choice but to point his direction. She abandoned her best friend Laney, still in mid-rant about the teetotalers who tried unsuccessfully to make this a dry party for the kids and moved toward Gunner as he watched her watching him.

Neither the magazine articles she had seen him in, nor the fights, both televised and live, had done justice to the changes time had wrought in Gunner. Staring at him with his brother was like looking into a window of her past. Asher was the gangly youth Gunner had been a decade before when she had trailed after her own brother and his handsome best friend. The boy who never seemed to notice her stood juxtaposed with the man he had become, the fighter he had grown into.

Both men had coal black hair; the younger man wore his spiked in a fashionable faux-hawk while the older brother slicked his back. The difference was in their eyes. Asher's were grey, like stone. They were fine eyes, but they were not Gunner's. His midnight blues held the stars for her and she wanted to be lost in them. Or she had before he left her and everything she offered him.

When Gunner rejected her and left town, it had served as a confirmation that he saw her the way everyone else did—the abominable snow witch. He was just too polite to say it. Before her brother took the pack, the wolves of Ushers Run openly viewed her as nothing more than a half-breed atrocity. She was born every bit the wolf her father and brother were but more. The other half was her mother, a snow witch who shifted into an owl. No one else in the pack had two animals to call. They probably still hated her for it behind closed doors. She thought Gunner appreciated her the way she was, but then he ran, too.

"Yeah, I know her." Gunner's eyes didn't leave hers when he said it.

"Come on, kid," Laney said as she grabbed Asher's hand and pulled him forward. "Let's go spike the eggnog and give these two some space." Asher followed like a lost puppy, no doubt lapping up every second of the attention he suddenly found himself receiving.

Noelle rolled her eyes before settling them back on Gunner. He looked like a changed man on the outside, all hard muscle, not the lean youth she remembered. The size he had grown into was overwhelming: six foot five with shoulders the width of a small car. If she didn't know for a fact that he was a werewolf she would have guessed his animal was a bear. He made her feel wonderfully small when he wasn't brooding like some kind of vengeful thunder god.

The teenage version of herself, who was somehow braver than this college-educated shadow she became, urged her to stand on her toes and taste him. Would his lips feel the same? When she kissed him last, he hadn't had the beard. She wanted to run her hands in his closely trimmed facial hair and draw him down to her. Enticing as the feeling was, she knew better than to take the chance with her heart. Appearances can change; what lay inside was another matter.

"Your friend wasn't very subtle." His voice rolled through her, like the stroke of fur against her skin. "It's been a long time, Noelle."

"Can we get some air?" she asked, her own voice coming out weak.

The corner of his mouth quirked up and he reached forward, past her cheek to the feather concealed in her hair behind her ear. Heat rose to her face at the casual touch. She fought back the overwhelming urge to nuzzle her cheek against his hand. As it was, her breath caught in a soft gasp. He let his hand drop and she instantly mourned the loss. Five minutes in this man's presence and she was already a sentimental schoolgirl. God help her.

"Let's do that." Gunner took her hand and led her through the press of inebriated partygoers who never saw her anyway. He took her outside through a pair of sliding glass doors to the back deck and the freedom of the cold night air—alone with the one man she always needed to see her.

Tonight Noelle wasn't sure she was ready to be seen, not after so long. Here in the dark she could hide the feelings poised to come rushing back after a decade of forced seclusion. She could admit to herself that she never had let go, not really. She dated in college to give the false pretense she had moved on. The men had mostly been human; no one she would consider forever. Through it all she kept that scrapbook, followed his career while she made her own.

Candles sat perched at random intervals along the railing of the raised patio area. Someone had taken the trouble to sweep it clear of this morning's fresh snowfall. The music followed them out into the night through her brother Ambrose's hidden sound system. He always did fancy his gadgets. She found it comfortable the way the melody filled the silence between them. "I'll Be Home for Christmas" began to play. The irony of that was not lost on her.

"Finally something good on his playlist," Noelle sighed.

Gunner eased her into his arms. He didn't ask, just carried on as though things were as they had been before that one night, and began to move to the slow holiday ballad that created its own spell for them. "It's not Bing Crosby, but it'll do. I can't stand that pop crap they try to pass as Christmas music."

"I remember. You never could," she admitted as she looked up in his eyes. "You're just jealous you know."

"Me? What do I have to be jealous of?" He asked it casually, so sure of himself as he looked down at her, searching for something.

She was glad he couldn't see her blush in the dark. "His voice. Michael Bublé could melt a brick with it." She left off that Gunner's was far more devastating.

Gunner laughed at her answer. She felt the rumble of it through to her toes, another piece of him she had forgotten to miss. Awareness flooded her, his touch was everywhere—the pressure of his hands steady on her waist, his voice caressing her in places he couldn't know, and his gaze, stripping her shields bare.

"You've changed, Noelle."

"How can you be sure?" she asked. "You've been gone ten years and back ten minutes." Her eyes met his and she did want to know what he saw. That lonely girl wanted to know if he saw her finally.

"You used to be this little bohemian girl, all flowing skirts and careless attitude." He paused and she glanced up at him, finding his gaze considerate, appraising. "You used to wear your feathers openly and not just one or two hidden in your hair. That's what I remember about you. Now you look so...polished. What do you do now?"

"You really want to know?" It surprised her that he would care. Not one letter in ten years. Dozens to her brother—she often handed him the mail—but never one to her.

"I really want to know."

Noelle pulled away and turned. She hugged herself as she moved to the rail overlooking flocked trees and the reflection of the moon on the frozen pond beyond that—unable to look at the lie in his eyes. She turned her face up to the sky. At least the stars were honest.

"Why'd you come home, Gunner? We're all doing fine here without you. Don't you have a title fight to go win or something?" Tears welled but she wouldn't let them go. He hadn't said anything wrong, not really.

"Asher needs me and eventually we all come home. It was just time."

A distant part of her, the hopeful girl that waited for him in that car and brazenly laid her heart out for him, had hoped for a different answer. But she wasn't surprised, not really. She was just Ambrose's little sister after all.

Why would he want her when he could have someone who was bred to mate a warrior? That's what he was, only his battlefield was a cage, where he had to control his beast and muzzle it while still fighting an opponent. That he did it at all fascinated her.

"We should go back to the party. I'm sure you're missed."

"I'm sure you're wrong," Noelle said, the words coming out harsher than she had intended. "Besides we haven't finished our dance."

It was a challenge more for her than him, she wouldn't let him see how he affected her. If he could hold back his beast, surely she could tame this useless desire that still burned for him. She turned back to him before she changed her mind and looked straight up into his eyes, willing a challenge in her own gaze, and wrapped her arms around his neck.

Gunner didn't touch her, instead he stared at the glass door behind her, stealing her bravado. When she turned and saw the source of his curtailed attention, irritation flared to anger. She caught someone's notice, just not the man she intended.

The metal of the door sliding open against the frame grated on her as Pierce stepped out onto the deck. His yellow eyes narrowed, his nostrils flaring as if he scented her emotions like a dog who didn't like it one bit. It was disrespectful at best in their current skin, but deep down it goaded her further. Pierce didn't really want her; he wanted the pack-leader's sister. She used him once to warm her bed when the loneliness threatened to swallow her and tonight she would pay the price.

The two men glared at one another, hackles raised as their baser instincts took over. They somehow resisted the change and stayed trapped in their human skin for the moment, but their posturing turned their behavior into something that resembled the animals beneath. Noelle looked from Pierce with his hate-filled eyes to Gunner and saw something she never thought to see. Was he truly jealous? She had to stop this before one of them turned.

She looked past Pierce to her brother, who stood beer in hand, looking ridiculous in his snowman sweater and quite pleased with himself. The smug bastard. He stepped out onto the deck and Noelle hoped he came to stop the fracas before it started.

Instead, Ambrose ambled to her side and leaned down

to casually whisper in her ear, "You can thank me later."

Gunner had no right to be jealous. He had walked away from her. No, he had run as fast as his collegiate scholarship could take him. But when Pierce walked out onto the deck and scented the air, they hadn't even needed words to hate each other. Over her.

How much had she changed in Gunner's absence? The things Pierce had said about her when they were young she couldn't possibly know. If she did, she wouldn't even entertain the idea of whatever relationship had formed between the two. That Ambrose had let her start something with Pierce, when her brother knew the vile crap the two-faced jackass said about her, made Gunner fume—Hell, the two had come to blows over it at one point. The dog-eyed bastard didn't deserve her.

He shouldn't have come home.

Noelle moved. Her head whipped around at something her brother had said and her cold eyes lit with an eerie green fire that marked her as separate from the rest of the pack. That difference terrified them and enthralled Gunner.

Wind that seemed to find its source in her emotions whipped the loose snow off the deck around her. It circled Noelle and Ambrose as if the air could draw a circle around the sibling standoff. In contrast to her seething agitation, her brother's posture was loose. His easy good-old boy smile quirked up one corner of his mouth, and he stood with one hand wrapped around a bottle of Bud Lite and the other hooked casually on the edge of his jeans pocket.

The glass doors shook as bodies pressed against it, eager for their entertainment. It was the reminder Gunner needed to leash the beast that had surged too close to the surface for comfort. He made his living off his control and here at her brother's house, in this spectacle of trashy clothes, he nearly lost it.

"Stop it," she said, her voice shrill. "Pierce, I don't know what you think you saw but you don't have the right—"

"I had the right when I marked you." Pierce spat the words and they felt like a blow.

She let that trash mark her? Gunner felt his claws slide free, contorting his hands before he clenched them tightly back into human fists. The pain bit deep in his hands and his heart.

Noelle's eyes flared brighter with her witch light, washing them all in their glow before dimming again. "You mean when you tried."

Those words eased Gunner. They were a relief, but not as much as the knowledge she was strong enough to fend off anyone she didn't want. He allowed himself to admit that, in a dark place in his heart, he worried that the witch in her might have made her too weak. But his concern hadn't made him stay. Why was Pierce behaving as if she was already his? He simply couldn't shake the small insidious voice of his doubt.

They were at an impasse, neither man wanted to step away and show weakness. Not in front of the pack-leader and not in front of her. With a frustrated growl of her own, she broke the stalemate.

"I've had enough of you both," she said, her voice strained with anger.

The snow moved faster, the wind whipping it up instead of in the slow circle it had been in, as if great wings beat against it. Noelle's arms spread wide as she flowed with her change. Hair smoothed into feathers and rushed rapidly down her body as she reformed. Her newly shaped wings, white and wide, pulsed against the air as she rose over them and then was gone, seeking freedom, and leaving them to sort out the mess.

"All right, show's over," Ambrose said to the crowd assembled at the door.

With a collective groan they began to disperse, leaving only the three men on the deck, one of whom Ambrose pointedly ignored. "Come on, Gunner," he said as he slapped his best friend on the back. "Let's get us some eggnog. I hear the mix just improved."

Chapter 2

Retail therapy, that's what Noelle needed or so Laney claimed the next day before dragging Noelle into town and trapping her in the hustle and bustle of Coral Ridge Mall. With the last minute gift-giving panic in full swing, the utter madness of thinking shopping could be therapeutic two days before Christmas was not lost on her.

The unique perfume of sweaty shoppers swathed in parkas warred with the scent of hot pretzels and overcooked meat from the food court. The commercial pop version of Christmas music being piped in to promote the shopping frenzy wasn't helping Noelle's mood either. It was enough to make her inner wolf twitchy and her owl molt from anxiety. Gunner was right. The classics were better, soothing, or maybe that's just when she was with him.

She rummaged through a rack of silk robes, not really seeing any of them. She wished she could be at work instead, wished for anywhere but here. An image of a roaring fire and naked flesh on a fur rug came to mind. She tramped it down—almost anywhere. Although the anthropology faculty of the University of Iowa was dismissed for winter break, she would have gone to her office, if Laney hadn't shown up.

Charlane Olsen, Laney to her friends, was another oddity in their small pack town. In a place where the women were taller than average, Laney towered over them at nearly six foot tall with honey blonde hair and chocolate eyes. You'd never guess she was a polar bear that had at seventeen moved south alone and petitioned for entrance into the wolf pack.

The elders told her no, but she never left and they didn't make her. Noelle and Laney found each other in their Contemporary Literature class. When the snow witch and the polar bear proceeded to tear apart the unsuspecting human teacher for not knowing who Truman Capote was, it was kismet. Noelle didn't know how she would have made it without Laney. Ambrose, Noelle's brother, must have known. And he valued loyalty above anything else. So after he finished his coup to take over the pack, he made room for both of them in the ranks.

"So what's the story with stud muffin last night?" Laney asked, interrupting the chaotic flow of Noelle's thoughts.

Laney was such a fixture in Noelle's life; she forgot sometimes that Laney didn't know what the problem was. She had transferred into school after Gunner had already graduated and left Noelle crushed.

"There isn't much to tell," Noelle said.

"Yeah, well I heard enough to know that's a bold-faced lie."

Noelle kept her breathing even. If she showed her reluctance to Laney, the were-bear would pounce. Noelle had to play it cool if she wanted out of this conversation. So she shrugged and tossed out a dig of her own. "You're one to talk, leading his kid brother away to spike the eggnog. He's sixteen."

Laney just laughed it off. "Someone has to teach the next generation and it's not like I let him have any. Besides one look at the two of you, your gooey eyes smoldering all over each other, well you really needed to get a room. Asher didn't need to see it. Had to protect the innocent. It's pack law." Laney tossed a red nightie trimmed in white feathers at Noelle.

She snatched the hanger and fabric from the air and glared at Laney. "We were not smoldering." Noelle gave the garment a quick glance. "And this is in no way large enough to cover anything."

"Me thinks the lady doth protest too much," Laney smirked, looking like she was sixteen instead of twenty-six in her ridiculous Care Bear t-shirt.

From the heat in Noelle's cheeks, she guessed she looked the same shade as the wadded up negligée in her hands. She glanced around the crowded store, tears of embarrassment burning in her eyes. Satisfied that no one was listening she leaned in and spilled out the truth. "Laney, I offered myself as his mate ten years ago. He didn't want me then; he doesn't want me now."

For a moment, Laney looked stricken. Considering what Noelle just shared, Laney likely hadn't anticipated the raw pain that she hadn't been able to mask from her words. Laney's eyes flicked up, past her friend. "Are you sure about that?"

Noelle nodded once, not trusting her voice.

"I'm not so sure." A slow smile spread across Laney's lips that had Noelle worried. The only thing worse than a curious Laney was a conniving Laney. Her friend nod-ded towards the dressing room. "Go try the nightie on."

"What are you up to?"

"Just do it, okay?" Laney made her eyes big and round, pleading like the sad puppy she wasn't.

Noelle sighed in resignation. "Fine, but whatever you're doing, you better not embarrass me."

How had Gunner let himself get talked into shopping two days before Christmas? Oh that's right, he was only supposed to drive Asher to the mall, which quickly turned into "as long as you're there." He glanced down at the list his mother had given him. Victoria's Secret was the last place he wanted to be, not with Noelle on his mind. There wasn't enough cold water in the county to cover the shower he would need to get over their slow dance from the night before. He shouldn't have done it, but being near Noelle like that in the dark, he had to have his hands on her. A slow dance was the only safe way he could do that and now with that memory like an open wound, he had to walk through this gauntlet.

Get the perfume his mother had sent him for and get out; that's all Gunner needed to do. But how would he make it before he started picturing Noelle in any of the tempting garments on display? He needed to get in and out fast. He shook his head. That was a poor choice of words, even in his head. Holding the list like a shield, he crossed the store threshold one carefully measured step at a time.

"Gunner, it's so nice to see you again." He turned to see an unusually tall blonde bounce toward him, around the racks that he was trying hard not to look at.

"I don't know you," he said, stating flatly what appeared obvious to him.

She didn't flinch. "Sure you do. Your kid brother helped me spike the eggnog last night. We weren't properly introduced." She held her hand out and he stared at it until she dropped it and shrugged. "I'm Noelle's friend Charlane, but everyone who wants to live calls me Laney."

"Then why'd you bother telling me your name is Charlane?" Gunner asked, even though he didn't really care.

He had to get on with this list and get out of the store.

Laney's eyebrows went up in surprise and then her curious gaze found his list and she smiled broadly. "You're a man on a mission. That explains so much. Let me see what it is you need and we'll get you out of here."

She snatched the list out of his grip and clutched his arm at the elbow, leading him further into this pink slice of hell. Where was a saleswoman to help him? How was this happening? He pummeled people in the face for a living, yet here he was being dragged through a lingerie store like a puppy on a leash. He did recall her now. She had done the same damn thing to Asher.

"What are you doing? I just need perfume," he protested when he discovered that his voice still worked. Table displays of lace panties and silk bras flew by. He closed his eyes against the onslaught as she continued to drag him.

"Don't worry about a thing. I got you covered." They reached the back of the store. She knocked on a door. "It's me, Laney."

He opening his eyes in time to see the door spring open and the crazy woman's smile turn wicked. "Merry Christmas. You can thank me later."

Before he had time to figure out what she meant. She handed him his list, shoved him through the open door and slammed it closed in his face. A familiar voice brushed through his mind like silk. "Laney, it's too small. I think I ripped the damn thing putting it on and I can't get it off without doing more damage."

He stared at Noelle in the gilded mirror that hung on the door. He'd have to be dead not to. Sheer red fabric hung loose from the form-fitting satin bodice. Its white feathered hem skimmed just below silky red panties.

"Wow." The word was spoken softly but in the quiet dressing room, it might as well have been a sonic boom.

It was like in an old black and white movie, both of them turning in slow motion, as if expecting to find an axe murderer or the ghost of Christmas past. Only when Gunner turned he locked eyes with a full color living fantasy. Noelle's perfect breasts were framed in red satin and white feathers. That was it. The dam of his resistance, the self-preserving wall that told him his best-friend and pack-leader's sister was off limits, had officially met its threshold.

Noelle's face and the swell of her breast flushed a furious red, like the fabric straining to cover her. The contrast of her creamy skin and her white blonde curls with those feathers made her look like a sinful angel.

Her whispered oath broke the moment. "I'm going to kill Laney."

Noelle had never been so thoroughly embarrassed in her life, at least not since that night in his Camaro. She didn't dare to linger on that now, not with Gunner standing there staring at her like he wanted to eat her for dessert. She had waited ten years for him to look at her like that. Why did it have to happen in the mall of all places? And he'd said "wow" with something like awe in his voice.

The simultaneous need to throw herself at him and crawl into a hole to die warred within her, but in the end, common sense won out. Laney put him in this position, too, and he was likely as mortified as she was.

"Close your eyes, please," she said, her voice clipped. She regretted the harshness in her words. "Just so you know, I'm not mad at you."

Gunner cleared his throat and shifted, as though he were uncomfortable. "I just came to buy something and got shoved in here. I'm so sorry." He held up a slim slip of paper that shook like a leaf as evidence. "You shouldn't be embarrassed. You're beautiful, you know." The explanation had come out in a rush but the last part—it had been deliberately slow. His tone hushed.

Noelle stilled in the act of pulling the filmy fabric up her torso to peel it off. "You don't mean that."

His eyes closed, Gunner's face furrowed in anger at her words. "You don't think you're beautiful? If you're with that fink, Pierce, he should be telling you that every day."

"I'm not with Pierce, not really." Her voice was a whisper as she watched the anger play across his features. Her hands dropped the fabric.

"I used to beat the hell out of that guy for the things he said." Gunner's voice was quiet and fierce. He crumpled the forgotten list in his hand. "I don't like you with him."

She reached up, wanting to stroke his beard, but hesitated. She was supposed to be changing not discussing her relationship with Pierce. Her hand hovered over his cheek. He had just walked in on her nearly naked. A state she was still in, but she was afraid to touch him. Wasn't this what she had wanted?

"Who's going to stand in his place? You? You didn't seem to want the honor before and eligible wolves are not exactly beating down my door."

"He wants you now because of your political value. But what if your brother fell from power, what if another coup happened? He'd cast you aside and you'd be vulnerable again," Gunner said, his voice a frustrated growl.

This was ridiculous. They were standing in a pink and white striped dressing room, jingle bells playing all around them, discussing love and werewolf politics.

She let her hand drop. Of course he didn't answer her. He had answered what he wanted her to ask, not her actual question. Shaking her head, she turned her back to him and pulled the negligée over her head. It was a tight squeeze to get it off and when it was done, she likely resembled a human candy cane with her nearly white hair, red face and the white sweater she tugged down over her midriff. It was a struggle in the confining space, to stuff herself back into her jeans and winter boots, but with grim determination, she managed it in record speed.

Noelle reached past Gunner for the door handle, intent on her escape, but his hand closed over hers. She looked up into his midnight eyes. When had he opened them? She never told him it was okay to look. He leaned down, lips hovering tantalizingly close to hers. All she had to do was go up an inch on her toes, maybe less. So close to tasting him. He smelled so good this close, like leather and burning wood.

"I'm not interested in politics, Noelle." His voice captured her in his thrall, like it always did. "I don't want to use you. I want to know you."

He said it last night too and she had taken it for a lie. What if it wasn't? Could her heart stand an afternoon with him to find out? She waited, willing him to ask. She couldn't be the one to make the move. She had laid too much on the line for this man already.

"Do you still skate?" he asked.

Of course she did. She had been skating since she could walk. But she held in her answer. Instead she tried to picture his hulking frame balanced on thin blades of metal. Intellectually she knew hockey players did it all the time, but not her fighter. This man who should have been a champion. He still could be one day.

"Yes, but..." Her voice came out meek. It seemed to be doing that a lot in his presence.

"So this mall still has a rink, right? Spend the rest of the afternoon with me."

He actually asked. She was so shocked she forgot to answer, until he started to pull away as if she had already rejected him. "But what about your list?"

He stopped, his gaze intent on her face as though he were trying to make out her thoughts. "Hang the list. Asher can do it tomorrow."

He really did want to go skating with her. "Okay."

"About damn time you two got it together," Laney called through the door.

Their hands still pressed together on the handle, they pushed down simultaneously and allowed the door to swing open. Laney stood holding her coat, a cheesy grin spread across her face. She wiggled her fingers at them in a silly wave, and then took off, leaving the pair of them alone to brave the walk of shame through the store. Disapproving glances were flung like arrows from customers and employees alike.

Noelle called after her. "Laney, when I get my hands on you..."

Chapter 3

"How long has it been since you went skating?" Noelle asked as she sat bent over, lacing the skates Gunner rented for her.

When he didn't answer she peered sideways at him. His skates were on and he sat hunched forward with his elbows braced on denim-clad knees. He stared at the ice on the other side of the glass, a grim expression written plainly across his features. He hadn't bothered with a coat over his navy thermal pullover today. She hadn't either. Werewolves rarely ever did unless concerned with appearances.

Noelle's concession to the cold that neither of them felt had been mint green knit gloves and a scarf. Her matching hat had a white poinsettia embellishment on the side. The hothouse flower had always been her favorite in all its varied colors, she wondered absently if he had ever noticed. Gunner's compromise had been brown leather gloves that were worn with age and a basic forest green skullcap. He was darkness to her light.

"Not since I was five," he answered at last, determination replacing the expression from a moment ago. "It's got to be like riding a bike though." He stood, hands out for balance, testing his substantial weight on the metal blades.

"Were you good at it then?" Noelle asked hopefully. "I don't recall."

Gunner took a tentative step and collapsed backwards, landing hard on the bench. Noelle covered her mouth with one gloved hand to restrain the giggle that threatened to break free.

He looked up at her with a grimace. "Not really."

Noelle walked to his side, balancing easily on her own skates. "Do you really want to do this? We can get hot cocoa and just talk somewhere. I'm okay with that."

"No," he said through gritted teeth. "You like to skate. I can do this. I just need some practice."

Noelle gripped the biceps of his left arm firmly, pulling him up until his arm pressed against her chest. God, she didn't remember his arm being so large and hard as stone. She met his dark hooded gaze and smiled warmly up at him. "Then let's just stick close until you get the hang of it."

He nodded his agreement and then they moved together, slow and steady. As they went out onto the ice, she tried to focus on balance, especially since he lacked it and outweighed her by nearly one hundred pounds. But the feel of his arm rubbing against her breasts as they moved had her pulse thrumming hot and heavy in her veins.

Noelle eased off, putting a little space between them and giving her bosom much needed breathing room. It was amazing how much the distance allowed her to notice. Instead of her world narrowed down to the points of contact between his body and hers, she could see the forest through the trees.

Teenagers whizzed by them, showboating for their friends. Noelle remembered the eternal quest for dominance among the hierarchy of the clique. In contrast, little kids and their parents clung desperately to the wall.

Their youthful giggles combined with the lively rhythm of "Jingle Bell Rock" fed into her buoyant mood.

A little girl's shriek of joy as her daddy swung her around on the ice drew Noelle's attention. Her father had done the same with her; she always assumed that by this age she would be doing the same with her own son or daughter. A decade ago, she hoped it would be with Gunner as her mate. As they made their first slow lap around the ice, he clung to her side as if she were his lifeline. Too bad she hadn't been his life line then.

"What are you thinking about?" Gunner asked her, interrupting the downward spiral of her thoughts. "You seem pretty intent on something."

She looked away as she answered him. "Just thinking about how things turned out differently than I had planned."

"Where did you plan to be?" The curiosity in his regard appeared genuine, but he had been the one who told her no and drove her home to her brother. Surely he knew the answer to this already.

"Mated with a child of my own," she said quietly, unable to look him in the eyes. "I would have still had my career. I don't think any of that would have changed, but I would have had a family."

The silence that followed told her Gunner hadn't thought about the past when he had asked. Her suspicion was confirmed when she glanced up and saw the grimace on his face. Had she been that easy to forget? Or was it something else? This doubt was making her sick like the bitter pill it was, churning in her stomach.

"So that you know, it wasn't that I didn't want you, Noelle."

Her eyebrows raised in surprise, and then she did her best to wipe her expression clean, careful to give away no other evidence of her emotions. He didn't shy away from the subject like she had assumed he would. She needed to keep herself in check. The fact that he was opening up to her like this didn't mean there was anything to hope for.

"Then I'd like to know what you meant by it because it sure seemed that way." Noelle's answer rushed out of her mouth before she had time to consider it. She thought he had her feelings on lock down but she couldn't keep the hurt from spilling out into her voice.

Noelle released his arm and skated ahead of him. For a quarter of an hour she had actually managed to forget, but he had to bring it all rushing back. Tears filled her eyes as she skated in silence. This had been a bad idea. Then she felt his hands on her waist, slowing her glide, and his chin rested on the top of her head. She should have slapped him away for the liberty he was taking, but damn if it didn't feel good to have him touch her instead of her reaching out for him.

"I wanted you then and I want you now." The low growling timbre of his voice rolled through her, touching her in her core. "Noelle, you were sixteen and my best friend's sister. I had a scholarship to get out of here. I couldn't give you the life you deserved if I stayed. I needed to build us a future."

Still moving forward with her back to him, Gunner pulled her flush against him until she felt the evidence of his arousal press into her behind. Her breathing hitched at the unexpected sensation. She had lain awake at night imagining just this, the hard length of him pressed against her and then inside of her. The taste of her long held desire thrilled her, but his words raised another question that she could not easily dismiss.

Noelle turned in the circle of his arms. "If that's true,

why did you wait ten years to come home?"

Gunner knew she was right. He never should have waited. It was clear to him now he had wasted all that time resisting her. They were too young to commit to a mating at sixteen and eighteen. He wasn't wrong about that, but he didn't have to mark her then. He could have slowed the pace down while they were both in school. If he hadn't been a hormonal idiot, clouded by the singular purpose to get out of town and away from his father's expectations, he might have.

"I had reasons, lots of them."

They glided in silence. Noelle continued to face him, skating backwards with effortless grace but clearly Gunner was slowing her down. He plodded along, gripping the wall as though his life depended on it. Toddlers were skating circles around them. He knew he should be embarrassed by that, but all that mattered was that she believed him and gave him the chance to make amends.

Gunner took a deep breath. He needed to tell her the reason that drove him to leave. "My father expected me to challenge your brother. He wanted me to lead the coup and I wouldn't do it."

Noelle's eyes went wide at Gunner's admission.

"There's more."

"More?" she echoed. He reached out to fold her in his arms, but she skated just out of reach and crossed her arms in front of herself.

Gunner pressed on, keen to get it out in the open at last. "My father thought your existence as a shifter witch was evidence of weakness in your family line and that you both needed to be erased. All he cared about was how we looked to the other packs. Image drove him. I couldn't do it. I never felt that way."

Noelle stared down at the ice. She turned away from Gunner, skating forward alone and he let her. Inept as he was, balanced on razor thin metal, it wasn't like he could catch her. She needed to process this. Gunner just wished she could do her thinking in his arms. He watched her pick up speed as she went, eyes closed, arms spread as if she was in her owl form instead of skating on the ice. She was magnificent in every form.

What would it be like to give her a family? He could buy the gym from his mother and stay permanently. He had enough money for that now. He hated giving up the fighting for good, but he would do it for her. He could almost picture a pack of children following behind her on the ice, his children, like a gaggle of cygnets behind a graceful swan. But did she still want him to mark her? There would be no going back if he did. And there was still Pierce; he claimed he had marked her, but she said she was free. Everything hinged on her. His life balanced more precariously than his hulking mass on these skates.

At last, she turned and skated back to him. He held his breath waiting on her verdict, praying she believed him.

Noelle moved in front of Gunner. Skating backwards once more, she hooked her arms around his neck. "Your loyalty was challenged." Her voice was hushed and her eyes, more green than blue, held something he had nearly given up on—trust.

"There wasn't another way," he admitted.

Gunner couldn't kill his best friend in a challenge, let alone the only girl in the world he had ever wanted. Even though a polished woman moved in his arms instead of the hippie witch with feathers in her hair, she was still the only woman for him. But he hadn't been able to move against his family either. So he had given up home, both this place and her, because she was his home just as surely as Ushers Run had ever been.

The world narrowed to this moment, his hands moved to her hips as they slowed to a stop on the ice. The ruined excuse for "White Christmas" blaring through the mall and the buzz of the other skaters moving around them, all seemed to fade away as he watched her lick her frosted pink lips in anticipation.

Eyes wide open, their lips grazed, testing. Noelle's head tilted and she pushed up on her toes as Gunner leaned down to capture her mouth with his own. He filled that kiss with all the suppressed need that had welled up behind the dam of his good intentions. She was soft and ready, parting her lips to accept him and he took what she offered, greedy for the taste of her, a tantalizing mix of vanilla and peppermint that was sweeter than any candy cane.

Gunner slid his hands around from her hips to the luscious curve of her ass that had teased him in those tiny red panties not even an hour ago. He ground the front of her into where he strained against the confining denim. When she swept her tongue through his mouth in answer to his own exploration of her and then quickly retreated, he growled his approval.

"Ewww, Mommy, those people are kissing!" a little voice called.

"Don't look, Timmy." The woman clapped her hand over the boy's eyes. "Get a room. There are kids here," she scolded before skating off with her child in tow.

Gunner was dimly aware of the woman and child in his peripheral vision as Noelle pulled back with a gasp that heralded the return of reality. Some Mariah Carey holiday knock off and the squawk of voices returned with a deafening roar. If only they were back in that dressing room instead of the ice. With the heat he was feeling, they should be standing in a puddle.

Skaters still turned all around them. Only now some of them were laughing and pointing. Gunner didn't mind; he never cared what anyone thought. His ability to tune out distraction was one of the tools in his arsenal that made him so dangerous in the cage. He was ready to put it to use by stealing another kiss, returning them to the inferno that still raged in his veins, that he could hear echoed in her own.

Noelle lowered her hands to his chest and leaned back to look up at him, their lower bodies still pressed to-gether. She opened her mouth to say something that turned into a shriek when she pitched suddenly forward. Gunner's balance was so tenuous that he was powerless to stop the momentum that pulled him down with her.

"Sorry," called a gangly youth as he skated away, too busy chasing after his friends to help them up. In Gunner's peripheral vision, the kid skated to the entrance gap on the far wall and snatched a folded up wad of cash before gliding away. Gunner only caught a quick glimpse, not enough to ID the man, before Noelle moved against him and his focus rushed back to her.

They lay in a heap on the ice, Noelle practically strad-dling Gunner. She sat up slowly, bracing her hands against his chest. When she sat back, the core of her rocked against him. It took a herculean effort not to grind his erection into her heated center. He swore it pulsed against him like a second heartbeat. Only layers of denim separated them, but considering they were in the middle of a crowded ice rink, they might as well have worn chastity belts. And when Gunner started he didn't intend to stop.

"Noelle?" he groaned.

Her eyes wore a cloud of lust-filled confusion. "Yes," she whispered.

"If you don't get off me, we're gonna have to find another dressing room."

Noelle's eyes went wide as she suddenly remembered where they were. She scrambled off Gunner's lap and he smothered a groan at her loss before dragging himself up onto his knees. Grabbing onto the wall with both hands, he hauled himself up. He cringed as he looked over his shoulder at her, but his concern quickly turned to surprise. Gunner expected to find her red faced and embarrassed, not smiling.

Eyes twinkling with a wicked gleam, she leaned into him. "I can do better than a dressing room."

Gunner's sharp intake of air was audible at her blatantly sexual tone. He waited for her to finish, afraid he would wake up and everything that had happened this afternoon would be gone.

"Come back to my cabin and we'll go for a run," Noelle said as she slowly glided backwards.

If God had any mercy, he hoped she was leading him to exit the ice, but he couldn't bring himself to break eye contact to check. He lurched forward, following her, trusting where she led him.

"You know my place," she whispered.

Gunner nodded, knowing that a possessive growl would come out instead of words.

Noelle reached the opening in the wall back to the row of benches. "Try to hurry, won't you? My wolf is restless."

Chapter 4

Gunner parked in front of Noelle's log cabin and killed the engine of his father's pristine white pickup truck. He had known about the place since she had it built on the edge of town two years ago. Ambrose slipped in those little nuggets about her in his letters. Gunner had devoured every one that came, hoping for another glimpse of Noelle through Ambrose's words.

As her big brother, Ambrose had never been able to deny Noelle anything, and with his construction company at his disposal, he built her dream home. So when she beckoned, Gunner knew just where to find her. But this was so much more than he had imagined.

It was like an idyllic holiday greeting card, the antique ones, with evergreen boughs swagged along the porch railings, punctuated with large red bows. White icicle lights lined the snow-covered eaves and her Christmas tree glowed invitingly with multicolored lights twinkling from her bay window. The woods behind the cabin were backlit by the moon's glow. The trees stood like tall sentinels, guarding her little piece of heaven.

He got out of the truck. The snow crunching beneath his feet was the only sound that broke the silence. He deposited his keys in the interior pocket of his open bomber jacket and touched the hidden velvet box with anticipation, needing the reminder that he was really here and this was really about to happen. He took the snow-dusted stairs two at a time.

When he ran home to get the ring, he started second-guessing himself. He changed his mind every other mile as he drove: was it too soon to make the kind of commitment she had wanted that night in his car or should he wait it out? Did she still want to spend her life as his mate? There was undeniable heat between them and history that ran deep.

Ultimately the linchpin of his decision was the horrible waste of time spent apart over the last decade. There was no shortage of things to learn about each other. The changes that came with the passage of years were waiting to be unearthed and he resolved not to waste another second. Now he only had to say the words.

An evergreen wreath bounced against the door as it flew open, his knuckles poised to knock still hanging in midair. "I thought you'd never get here." Noelle grabbed the lapel of his jacket and hauled him inside. "What took you so long?"

"I had to pick something up on my way," Gunner answered, remaining purposely obtuse.

He leaned down to steal a kiss but she backed away quickly with a playful smile. A low growl rumbled through him. He stalked towards her, excited for the game of chase she was hinting at.

"Down, boy," Noelle teased. "Make yourself at home for a few minutes and I'll be right back." The warm glint in her eyes, more blue then green today like a winter sky, enticed him, making his blood rush as if the chase had already started. The potent mix of sensual energy mingled with her playful attitude called out to him as she sashayed down the hall away from him, barefoot and wrapped in a long terrycloth bathrobe.

Without the distraction of her in the room, he saw it for the first time. A plush sofa faced the stacked stone fireplace, the fire already crackling and casting a soft glow on the space. Evergreen boughs and red taper candles flickered softly from their place on the mantle. Two old school red and white stockings dangled from hooks on either end. "Ambrose" was stitched in gold thread on one and "Noelle" on the other.

Gunner moved to the built-in bookcase beside the fireplace, hoping its contents would give him an added window into the woman he left behind. A selection of historical romances lined a lower shelf, occasionally broken up by framed photos. He picked up the one with Noelle and Laney smiling in their cap and gown. He ran his fingers over the image as if he could somehow will himself into the moment he missed.

The day Gunner received the letter from Ambrose about her graduation was the first day Gunner found satisfaction in a punching bag. He had been so angry about missing another milestone in her life; he had needed an outlet to work out his frustration. He spent an hour punishing a punching bag, and when he turned around, he found an audience. The man who would become his trainer spent the rest of that evening convincing Gunner to give up wrestling and try Mixed Martial Arts instead. In one way or another, Noelle had influenced every change he made in his life.

Placing the silver frame back in its home on the shelf, Gunner spotted a row of scrapbooks. Eager to see more of the life he missed, he pulled the first one off the shelf and cracked the large square volume open. The first page was an article with no photos. He scanned the evenly typeset words slowly, expecting to find some proof of her academic life but was shocked to discover an article on his first colligate wrestling tournament.

Gunner flipped through the rest of the book, and found

page after page of his athletic exploits. The Olympic wrestling team tryouts, his first cage fight, and the sports drink ad he'd done clipped carefully from a magazine; it was all there. Towards the back of the book, he discovered selfies of her with arenas in the background and ticket stubs for fight cards he had been on. One shot was of him throwing a punch in the cage. It was not a promotional photo. This appeared to come from her camera.

While he had been worried about Noelle, gleaning little bits of her life from letters, she had been right there, keeping tabs on him while remaining just out of reach. Noelle had been in the same building with him not even a month ago when he won his seat as the number one contender for the middleweight belt. It kindled hope deep inside him; perhaps there was still a chance for them and not just long suppressed lust. She might say yes.

"You weren't supposed to see that," Noelle whispered, breaking his reverie.

One moment's stupidity, forgetting to put away the scrapbook, would cost Noelle dearly. She wanted to cry. She had given up on ever being with Gunner, be it for one night or forever, or thought she had until the magic from the ice rink. And although she was a witch, she did not stoop to magic for love. She would never demean herself that far. He would take her or leave her without interference, as it should be.

The book snapped shut and she flinched. Any time now, Gunner was going to call her a crazy stalker and walk out that door. She closed her eyes against the sound she expected to hear next, her front door slamming. Seconds passed, her heart racing, blood thundering in her ears. She couldn't stand here any longer waiting for the condemnation that was coming. Waiting for him to say or do something to fill the silence.

There was no reason to stand here and wait for his anger like the lovesick teenager she once was. Her rapidly rising anxiety whispered another solution—run. All she had to do was let go and this could all go away, at least for the moment.

Noelle tugged at the loose belt that tied the robe closed and shrugged the garment from her shoulders, allowing it to drop into a pool of white at her feet. She reached deep for the wolf that prowled within her, whispering to her inner beast that it was time to run. The chill that served as her wolf's answer raced through Noelle as if she stood in a snowdrift instead of fluffy terry cloth.

Then the chill in her human limbs turned to fire as she went down on her hands and knees. The wolf change was different from shifting to an owl. Her owl was simply a shape she melted into like a costume and mask. Her wolf was a twin soul to her own, sharing a deeper bond that slumbered until it had its turn to play. A flood of adrenaline ripped apart her body, splitting apart skin and realigning bones. In the ebb that followed, what little pain there had been was carried away, leaving her reformed. The day she learned to let it wash over her, to let the wolf have her chance, the pain became manageable. Today she was using her beast to escape.

Noelle's wolf-self shook like a wet dog and then trotted down the hall to the kitchen. There lay the means to breakout. In her human shape, she had been removing the magic ward over the large dog door that kept anyone but her from passing through, while Gunner had been perusing the damning evidence.

"Where are you going?" Gunner's voice cut through her, closer than she had imagined.

Her wolf-self looked back, giving Noelle a moment to assess. He stalked towards her, still in his human skin, but little else. A trail of clothes littered the floor, leaving him very naked. Noelle wanted to linger over the black lines of ink carved into his shoulder and ribs. She had waited ten years to see the hard lines of this man's body. Her wolf-self was not impressed; she wanted the wolf inside that skin to come out.

If he wasn't leaving, Gunner must be expecting answers. Noelle would too if she stood in his place. Frustration and determination coursed through her souls. She would not make it easy. Noelle nudged her wolf-self to suggest she flee before he finished his change. The wolf-self was having none of it. Feeding on Noelle's base human emotions, the beast woke up in heat and wanted to play.

The she-wolf yipped at him and looked pointedly at the kitchen door. Gunner's eyes narrowed on her as he knelt on the floor. Noelle dove through the dog door and let it close with a heavy *thwap* behind her. She did not wait to watch his change. The chase was on after all.

The cool air enveloped Noelle, welcoming her into the night. She leapt off the back porch stairs into the snow. Sinking up to her chest in the recently laid ground cover, the chill bit through her fur, cooling the rush of hormones. An alpha male was in her kitchen and if she wanted to get away, she needed her head.

Noelle's beast raised her muzzle to the sky, calling out in supplication to the night. The chorus of nature with its myriad instruments—rang from the wind rushing through skeletal branches to the owls' hoots blended with the beating of wings; the night music stilled as if waiting with bated breath. An answering howl echoed from inside the cabin walls, shaking the windows that pretended to contain it.

It was like the bell that called the start to one of Gunner's fights, only now it called her to action. Noelle bounded into the chest-deep snow. Her only advantage was to stay in the deep snow and use it like camouflage for the white fur of her arctic wolf form. With the trail and scent markings that she could not avoid leaving behind, it was her best defense. She weaved in and out of trees, picking up speed as she went.

Circling around, she slowed to a prowl, listening for his chase. She saw his massive black head, his nose to the ground tracking her scent. Now her wolf-self was interested. Noelle wanted to run away but her wolf-self wanted to get closer, to let him know she was there for the chase, or so her human side believed. Moving downwind, she inched closer to watch him. But his head snapped up and grey eyes locked on her.

The she-wolf moved in: why be chased if she could have him now? Noelle was growing restless inside the wolf. The beast had her own agenda and would not move away. Gunner's head cocked to the side, watching her come. The two wolves, black and white, like day and night, circled each other.

Her mate—Noelle realized her wolf-self made the choice for her. She whispered to her animal soul, *he is not for us*. But Noelle felt it. Her other self would not be pacified. She had chosen and he had answered her call. Too bad the human within the great black beast would not follow. His wolf nuzzled the neck of the arctic female.

Noelle's wolf-self was content. She receded, quietly

and with little fanfare, catching Noelle off guard and leaving her huddled naked and shivering in the snow. The reverse change was not so violent and painful. Indeed, Noelle often found it anti-climactic. The chill of the snow was startling but not as startling as what her wolf-self had done. Her beast was dumping her out of the frying pan and into the fire, telling her in no uncertain terms, *get your shit together girl and get our mate.*

Gunner's wolf stared down at the shivering naked woman at his feet. One moment he had been scenting his mate, negotiating a pair bond, and the next Noelle was dumped unceremoniously by her other nature into the snow. She scrambled up on all fours as though her body had not changed. Noelle backed away slowly, teeth chattering. The woman did not trust him the way the she-wolf had.

Pulling herself up to her feet she did not try to hide her fragile nude form. Like a Viking shield maiden, she squared her shoulders and moved back toward the cabin, walking barefoot in the snow as if she felt nothing. "I know you're mad at me, but I can explain," she said.

There was nothing to explain, at least not as far as Gunner or the wolf were concerned. She had tracked them, stayed with them, through the decade he had thought lost. She would never be a boring mate; she would be a strong one.

"I know you told me to let you go, but I couldn't." She reached the steps and began to back up slowly. "You see those letters to my brother—they taunted me. You told Ambrose how you were doing but I had no clue. I just wanted to know and he wouldn't tell me."

His wolf stalked forward as her hands grasped the brass handle on the back door. His gaze bounced from her hand to the silent tears rolling down her face.

"I'm not a crazy stalker. I mean after seeing my book, you probably think so, but I'm not. I never hacked you or anything scary like that. I just…" Noelle's voice faltered. "I just wanted to know that you were okay. All that fighting and no pack. I worried. So now you know why." Her voice hardened and she looked away, as though preparing to flee or bracing for him to.

That was it; she thought he was going to leave her again. If she had only given him a chance to tell her how much it meant that she still cared to follow him. That she still felt something for him that went beyond lust. He should have told her before she could run, but then she dropped that robe and the first glimpse of her pale beauty, naked before him as she was now had shorted his mind into stunned silence.

Gunner's beast released him, *it's time to tell her and claim our mate.* Gunner felt the pressure of his body expanding to the proportions it normally held as the wolf receded and went back into its slumber. He knelt on the snow clad only in his human skin, packed where their animals had circled each other moments before.

The growl in his voice rumbled with his promise. "I'm not walking away again."

Chapter 5

Gripping the door handle, the cold bite of wood pressed into Noelle's back. She stood frozen in place. The slow burn that Gunner stoked inside her chased away the cold that should have concerned her. The sight of beautiful naked man stalking up the porch stairs coupled with the continuous loop of his words playing back in her mind caused the heat to spread out from her core to her limbs.

Noelle's wolf-self had not been interested in giving her more than a glimpse before. Now she had free rein to linger over the peaks and valleys of his chiseled physique, honed like an artist with marble block into a masterpiece made for endurance and combat. Noelle had seen him bare-chested in the octagon when he fought and had glimpsed the tattoo inked onto his side, like a fresco into plaster. However, she'd never been close enough to make out details beyond a depiction of a moonlit forest-scape and a howling wolf.

"Don't look so concerned. You have no idea what cold snow does to a man," Gunner said from the top step just feet from her.

"That wasn't what I was looking at." Noelle's eyes flickered down and heat flooded her cheeks. "But now that you mention it, if the cold and snow have somehow diminished you, then I am curious to see you warm. As you are, you've nothing to be ashamed of."

Noelle reached out, fingers grazing the snow owl silhouetted against the moon on his skin, tracing its outline. In his own way, he carried her with him, just as she had with that scrapbook. If he felt embarrassed by her discovery, as she had been of him finding her scrapbook, he masked it. His dark sapphire eyes were steady as they met hers.

"I couldn't fight without you by my side." Gunner reached up, trailing his fingers across her flaming cheeks. "It's too bad I didn't know that I wasn't."

"I thought..." Her words came out little more than a whisper that dissolved when he moved forward and the hard length of his body pressed into her softness.

Gunner's hand moved from her cheek and burrowed into her curls to stroke the sensitive skin at her nape with his knuckle. Lacking courage, Noelle leashed the impulse to turn her face into his hand and kiss the inside of his wrist.

"You don't know how bad I wanted to come back for you. I suffered thinking you hated me, Noelle. I hated myself. Why would your brother let you anywhere near me, let alone allow me to be your mate?"

Gunner rested his hands on the doorframe to cage her loosely in his embrace. He bent his head and grazed the vulnerable column of her throat with his lips. That simple touch ached in her beaded nipples, hardened by the mixture of cold and the desire thrumming through her like a second heartbeat much lower.

"Ambrose would have allowed it because I loved you," Noelle said, her voice breathless.

Gunner paused, his lips hovering over her pulse. "Loved? Am I too late? It didn't feel like it was too late when we were on the ice." His hand left the doorframe to cup her. One finger burned a trail down her stomach and then slid against her moist heat, stealing a strangled gasp from her. "It doesn't feel like I'm too late now either."

His free hand closed over hers, as it had in the dressing room earlier. She blushed at the memory of him seeing her in that negligée. Had that only been this afternoon? Now she stood bare and pressed against his nude body, balanced on the precipice of everything she ever wanted. Now and in that dressing room she had been meek. But that wasn't what she wanted to be. She wanted to be brazen and confident the way she had been on the ice, the way she had been ten years before.

Her wolf-self whispered to her. She closed her eyes to him and pictured the push and pull of their awkward romance. She was certain the answer to her troubled heart lay somewhere in their mistakes. When she had thrown herself at him all those years ago, she had been the aggressor and he ran away. Her eyes flew open and she smiled up at him. Gunner was an alpha wolf, not just a man. He needed the chase.

Turning the knob, Noelle allowed the door to swing inward. She went with the momentum, pulling from his hands and allowing her instinct to take hold. Noelle did as the she-wolf within her instructed. Noelle ran. This time, rather than running in shame from him, she ran with anticipation of her impending pleasure. She heard the growl behind her. The corners of her lips hitched up with the certainty that she was right.

Noelle looked back at Gunner; he caught himself against the doorframe. A wicked feral grin split across his handsome face and she wanted everything that it promised. He launched himself forward. The door slammed shut behind him as she rounded the corner into the living room. She caught a glimpse of his human feet skidding on the tile, slick from the snow they had tracked in. She didn't stop, couldn't stop until he caught her. Noelle offered a silent prayer that it would be over soon, ending both their misery.

Noelle ran between the sofa and the fire, thinking to circle and keep the furniture between them. He must have counted on that because when she looked back again, he wasn't behind her. She ran straight into his arms.

"Why are you always running?" Gunner's tone was rife with amusement.

Heart pounding, she let her gaze sweep up his broad chest with its dusting of dark hair. Her hands followed where her eyes led, until her fingers found the scruff of his close-cut beard. It was soft and she wondered what it would feel like in her most sensitive places. "I'm just waiting to be caught."

The spark in his midnight blue eyes warmed her down to her toes. His heated lips crashed into hers, snaring her irrevocably. Her knees gave out with the intensity of it, but he held her rock steady as he lowered her to the floor. His kiss was a savage invasion and she reveled in it, tempting him forward with a playful teasing of her own tongue.

Gunner's hands spanned her rib cage and stroked upward to caress her breasts. His thumbs teased the hard pearls of her nipples. Her arms snaked around his neck to hold on for dear life as the pleasure of his wandering hands rocketed through her. She ached for more. When his lips left hers and began to explore she wanted to cry with frustration. Their earlier exploits had worked her to such a pitch that the long tease he was promising held no appeal. Hoping to shift the pace, she let go of his neck and let her hand trail down between them until she found the hard length of him.

The hiss of Gunner's sharp intake of breath added to her blossoming courage. "What are you doing?" he barked, his voice filled with a strain that matched her own.

Calling up the reserves of the heedless abandon with which she had run, Noelle suppressed the awkwardness that had ruled her and spread her thighs in invitation. "Take your time later. I want you now."

Gunner moved to kneel in the space she opened for him with a torturous measured pace. He loomed over her, poised at her opening. She felt the tip of him enter her.

"Is this what you wanted?" he teased.

In answer, Noelle wrapped her legs around his waist and attempted to thrust forward and take more of him. His hand on her hip pinned her in place.

"Tell me," he growled.

"Yes!" she cried out, desperate for the friction to start.

Gunner rewarded her with another delicious inch and she moaned in pleasure tinged with her mounting need. He leaned closer, giving her more of himself. He licked the soft spot between her neck and shoulder, causing her to buck beneath him from the intensity of her pleasure. He pulled back the length she gained.

He nipped at the spot he had laved with his tongue. "What about this, Noelle? Do you want my mark?"

She stilled beneath him and he started to pull away. Noelle locked her ankles at the small of his back and reached up to pull him down to her. "No, don't leave me, Gunner. I want it." Heaven help her, she meant it. Even with the chase, Noelle thought only that he'd make love to her, not offer the very thing he'd denied her in the past.

"You have to be sure." The playful banter had gone out of his tone. "I can't take it back when I'm done."

Christmas lights from the tree behind her reflected in his eyes like the stars in the deep blue of night, as if she was staring up at the firmament. Noelle saw in their depths that he was afraid. This was her chance to pay him back for the rejection he put her through a decade before. Their roles were reversed and although he was in a seemingly dominant position, he had handed her the keys to say no and break him. The power of it brought tears to her eyes.

"Yes," Noelle whispered. "I want it. I claim you." She turned her head, offering up the sensitive flesh.

"And I claim you." Gunner thrust home while biting down, the pleasure easing the momentary sting.

His teeth clamped on to her as he rocked, beginning the rhythm that made her forget her name, let alone the discomfort. He released the mark and kissed it. His beard rasped against the now raw evidence that she was his partner and no one else's.

The undulating pace that he set became broken and frantic as she rose up to meet him. Her pleasure built with his frenzied need. He reached between them and found her sensitive spot, just above where they joined, it was her undoing and she crashed into her finish, made punishing from long denied need.

"God," she moaned, when she came down, her body still humming like a tuning fork that had found its pitch. "It feels like I've been flying."

Gunner nuzzled her ear as his weight collapsed onto her, their bodies still joined. His lips pulled into a smile that she could feel against her neck. "I found your feathers."

Contentment filled Gunner to the brim. Rolling to the side, he pulled Noelle with him so that she draped across his chest in a boneless heap. Her red-lacquered nails trailed lazy circles around the moon inked onto his ribs. The heat from the fire they ended up in front of seeped into his skin. The snap and crackle as it burned kept the silence at bay and added to the languid feeling that settled in his limbs.

They'd landed on the rug in front of the fire, nearly underneath the Christmas tree. He stared up at the blown-glass ornaments, with their colorful depictions of birds and leaping reindeer. He even spotted the glass pickle hidden further back within the branches. He liked the handmade ornaments best. Noelle had hung oranges, bound by ribbon, and pierced with whole cloves to make them fragrant. Popcorn threaded with string wound around the tree as garland. The traditional touches made her tree special.

To Gunner, that was how you should keep Christmas. That's how it had been with his grandparents. His father, on the other hand, had always made his mom do whatever the trend was. The Thoren family had to keep up appearances and everyone had better conform to his standard.

"I have to have the feathers," Noelle said. The contented cadence of her tone pulled his mind back from its meandering, to focus on her. "They're part of my change—part of the magic."

He considered her words as he lifted one of her nearly white curls to twirl in his fingers. "So if I let you put feathers in my hair, I could change too?"

"No," she answered looking up at him. Her pale green-blue eyes shone like beacons. "It isn't that simple. It is still inherent in my magic, but it needs a focus that I pull around me. I wear the spell like a coat that only fits me."

"That explains why your clothes shift with you as an owl. It's damn convenient." Gunner paused, weighing if it was too soon for this question. They were mated, but they still had ground to cover between them and he didn't want to upset the peace that had settled into this moment. Deciding to risk it, he forged ahead. "Will our children be both owl and wolf?"

Noelle sat up, pulling away as she did.

He watched her move, anxious to see her expression. When she turned to face him, he cursed his eagerness to delve into the sensitive subject. Her lips pressed into a thin line and the joy that had been in her eyes a moment ago was gone. Seeing that raw pain made him want to go out and pound on every wolf that had ever taunted her as the abominable snow witch.

"Why do you ask?" Her tone was cautious as she moved to kneel beside him, creating distance between them that he didn't like.

"We didn't exactly prevent a litter just now," he said, projecting a casual ease to mask his concern for her feelings. "And it would be good if our children were like you."

The breath she had been holding rushed out and the subtle lines of tension that had developed around her eyes relaxed and were replaced by the unshed shimmer of tears. "I thought that was why you turned me down before. Because of what I am, but then when you told me about your father and I saw your tattoo I started to hope..."

"I'm home now. With you. I took over the gym so I won't need to fight anymore. I'm not leaving you again."

Her eye's widened. She reached out with shaking fingers, gripping his shoulder. "Gunner, you don't have too..."

Gunner sat up and reached for the jacket hanging from the edge of the sofa, where he cast it off chasing her. He pulled out the red velvet box secreted within. When he opened it, her jaw went slack and her hands flew up to cover her gaping mouth. Marquee-cut garnets formed a circle around a one-carat diamond and the thin yellow gold band it balanced on sparkled with small inset diamonds. It was custom-designed to look like a poinsettia.

"I had it made when your brother told me you graduated college. I wanted to come back then." Gunner took it out of the box and slid it down the third finger of her shaking left hand. "My mark makes us forever...but I want the whole world to know it. Not just the wolves."

The sound of a car door slamming broke apart the moment. Gunner growled at the interruption. The moment had come; Noelle was his and he couldn't even get through it.

A forced sounding burble of nervous laughter escaped Noelle as she scrambled up off the floor and tossed Gunner his pants. "It's probably just Ambrose. I'll try and get him to go away but just in case he won't take the hint, you should probably go down to the bathroom at the end of the hall and get decent."

She bent down to snatch up her robe, giving him a full view of her heavy breasts. God, he wanted her. Couldn't wait to hear her say yes. He prowled across the floor toward her as she pulled the white terry cloth over her shoulders.

"You didn't answer me, Noelle." He brushed back her

white blonde curls to kiss the tender red flesh of his mark above her collarbone.

Noelle pushed him back and pulled the fluffy collar of her robe closed tighter to cover the sign of their mating. Gunner frowned. She turned away and began gathering his discarded clothing into her arms. Shoving the wadded load at him, she ushered him down the hall.

"Go on, I'll take care of this. Just don't come out or I'll never get rid of him." She said as she hustled him into the bathroom and slammed the door in his face.

Gunner listened to her moving down the hall as he pulled on his jeans. He couldn't help but feel doubt creep in. Mated after a decade of separation, this should be the most romantic moment of their lives and it had been until they heard the car outside. Gunner had so many questions. Hadn't they both wanted this? Why did she hide his mark? It was something to be proud of, but she covered it and refused to answer him. That silence was breaking him down.

For her to be acting this way she must fear Ambrose's reaction to the mating. That was a puzzle all its own. Gunner had been on good terms with the pack leader, her half-brother, since he left. The man was like Gunner's own brother. They'd written each other and Ambrose had even told him small things about Noelle. Ambrose had never said his sister was off limits; Gunner had put that restriction on himself.

Fuck, Ambrose. He was going to find out Gunner was his brother-in-law soon enough.

Gunner opened the bathroom door and took a step out into the hall as he hastily pulled his navy thermal back over his head. The male voice that met his ears had him stopping short.

"Where the hell are you hiding him, Noelle?" Pierce

Mathison's gruff tone met Gunner like a blow to the solar plexus. A slow fire of anger began churning inside Gunner. His wolf soul raged at him to tear down the hall and put the alpha wannabe in his place.

"Please just go. He isn't here. He went for a run in the woods." Her lie held Gunner back once more. As her mate it was Gunner's place to defend her and her home. He didn't know what any of this meant, but he was sure as hell going to ask her.

Chapter 6

Noelle's own impatience was ruining her life.

This should have been the happiest moment of her life. Instead, she was mortified. Not at Gunner—she waited a decade to be his mate. Now she was and he had a ring made just for her. He wanted the public, his fight fans, to know he had a wife. But the one night drunken indiscretion that had served as a balm to her loneliness was intruding on her forever.

"I saw you suckin' face with him in the mall," Pierce slurred as he pushed his way past the front door, his nose and eyes a red stain on his pallid face. "You screwin' him now?"

"It's none of your business. Now get out of my house," Noelle said. She gripped the collar of her robe, keeping it high.

"Bullshit. It became my business when you took me home."

God, she hoped Gunner hadn't heard that. Who was she kidding? He was probably in the bathroom hanging on every word. Noelle winced at the idea. What she didn't want to happen was for Gunner to go all alpha male and storm out here. She did not need two male wolves brawling over her in the living room. Noelle messed this up and now she had to make Pierce go away before Gunner decided she wasn't worthy to be his mate after all.

"Pierce, you're drunk. I'm not your mate and you have no claim here. Just go." Reason with him. That's all she needed to do: be reasonable. If it could only be that easy.

Pierce paced in front of the door. When he turned to leave, his shoulders slumped in apparent defeat, Noelle let out her breathe in a rush. Then he looked up, his eyes seeing the white truck parked off to the side. "You buy a new truck?"

When Noelle didn't answer, Pierce turned, red-rimmed eyes dark with anger as they swept the room beyond her shoulders. There would be nothing to see but a fire dwindling from neglect. She'd gotten every scrap of clothes off the floor and if Pierce would just leave she'd get back to the naked man they belonged to.

A piece of her that was steadily getting louder worried about Gunner and the silence from down the hall. What was he thinking about all of this? A mating pair bound could be a powerful biological urge, meant to last forever, but separations happened. Her own mother and father were proof of that. They came back together, unable to resist the pull to be with their mate, but the idea of losing Gunner for another decade made her skin crawl. The need to fix this pounded in her temples.

Pierce's stare fixed on one spot at the edge of her sofa. For a full minute, she resisted the urge to look, knowing on instinct, when she did look, it would be bad. Turning slowly, she rolled her shoulders, like a fighter bracing for round two and then she looked. It was just a shoe, or rather the toe of a shoe. Problem was, it wasn't a woman's shoe.

Shoving the door wide, Pierce forced Noelle to step back or be hit. "Where you hidin' that muscle-bound freak?"

Pierce stomped down the hall and threw open the door

to her bedroom—empty. But she knew that. She had to remain calm. If she did, he would give up and go away. She just had to wait him out. Locking down her emotions, she didn't flinch when Pierce flung open the closet door with a bang. He reached in sweeping the clothes to the side as if Gunner would ever hide there.

Pierce turned on her with a frustrated growl. "Tell me where."

She stood blocking the door to the bathroom, her heart in her throat. "Get out of my house before I call Ambrose. I doubt he'd appreciate you harassing his kid sister."

If she thought the drunk idiot was unhinged before, she was wrong. Of all things, that threat snapped his leash. Pierce shoved her and she stumbled back over the edge of the hall rug and rammed into the wall with her shoulder. With a feral cry that was part scream and part growl, she lunged at Pierce as he burst past her into the bathroom where she stowed Gunner. It too was empty and had Pierce looked at her she was sure his dumbfounded expression matched her own.

For a moment relief poured out of her like steam from a kettle. Gunner must have gone out a window. It didn't seem like him, but it explained why he hadn't come out ready to kill Pierce. If Gunner wasn't there, he hadn't heard the awful things Pierce said. It was a conversation they needed to have but it could still happen on her terms.

Noelle's wolf was awake now, prowling in the pit of her stomach and watching through her eyes, anxious to take over and dispose of the threat. The ambient green-blue glow of her eyes lit the dark corners of the bathroom they stood in. The wolf might be ready to defend but the witch was seething with suppressed rage and anxiety.

She made it nine years without Gunner. Not so much

as a date to a movie. Nothing tempted her. Then she watched the fights at the local bar. Gunner wasn't fighting that night otherwise she would have traveled, but watching all those hard bodies…. The fights always got her going, add alcohol to fuel the fire and it became a cocktail for a colossal mistake. By the time Pierce made it back to her house she was sober enough to know it was wrong and just enough to keep him from marking her, but not enough to stop. God help her.

Pierce didn't fear her wolf; no one feared the little white arctic she-wolf. But he did fear the witch and those eyes sent him scrambling back down the hall. "Ellie, honey, calm down."

"My name is not Ellie and I am not now nor will I ever be your honey." The words came out low and ominous, like a slow leak of gas right before the spark set off the inferno. "This is the last time I'm gonna say it, Pierce. Get out of my house."

Whatever he saw in her face, he didn't question. He just backpedaled for the door. "This isn't over. I'm gonna find him. That's the great thing about small towns. When I do, he's gonna be sorry for touching what ain't his." They were tough words for a man who looked like he wanted to piss himself.

She knew it was about saving face now and he would not stop; it was the nature of the wolf. They fought for territory and she was it. With nothing further to say and no Gunner to confront, he strode out the door, having sobered enough to walk a little straighter then he had on the way in. She closed the door behind Pierce with a soft click and sank to the floor. The tension that held her up through it all having escaped like helium from a balloon.

With her eyes closed, she rested her forehead on the

cool glass of her front door.

"Show me where he marked you, Noelle." Gunner's deep voice bristled with the emotion she imagined must be simmering under that handsome-as-sin exterior.

And to think, for a moment, Noelle had suffered under the delusion that maybe he hadn't heard any of that jackass' rambling. She should have known she wasn't that lucky. This was not how her happily ever after was supposed to be. Noelle turned her back against the door. She pushed herself up off the floor.

Gunner stood with the open basement door to his back with his bare feet planted wide, wearing just his jeans, navy thermal shirt, and a whole lot of rage. His hands clenched and unclenched as if they ached to be tearing into something or someone. The charge in the room told her his change was as close as hers had been if not closer.

"There isn't a mark." Noelle's voice was as frail as she felt inside.

"I heard him," Gunner said, his words clipped to restrain the anger that had begun to grow with every word he heard through the door. "No man is that possessive over a one off piece of tail unless he believes he's a mated wolf."

Noelle looked away sharply, her eyes narrowed. She crossed her arms in front of herself, rubbing absently, as if to soothe her ruffled emotions. "He claimed to Ambrose that he did mark me, but he didn't and Ambrose won't recognize it. My brother will recognize us."

"Where?" Gunner asked again. His heart seemed to beat faster with each denial she made. If Pierce really had marked her, then Gunner was the trespasser and he could not bear the thought of losing her now. Of course, if he kept pushing Noelle like this, she might give up on Gunner. The idea of it made his blood run cold.

"Stop. There's only you now." Noelle's voice was full of unshed tears. The blue, green and red lights from the tree reflected off the watery veil over her aquamarine eyes that he loved. "I did a dumb thing and slept with him. One time. I never let him mark me."

Gunner's heart burned with conflict. He wanted to believe her—needed to. From the outside looking in, everything about this looked wrong. Appearances—his life always seemed to come down to that. "Tell me why?" he asked at last.

"You said it yourself. To him I am nothing more than a political advantage. He caught me at a low moment when I just needed to be..." Noelle's voice trailed off, her eyes averted. When she answered, her voice was a whisper that struck him sharply. "Filled—I needed to chase the emptiness away and I did it the wrong way."

What had he done to them, pushing her away for ten years? He drove her into the arms of a scheming, drunken waste of fur, and he was paying steeply for his foolish belief that he needed to leave for them all. If he had only stood for what was right—against his father— he would not be losing her to the werewolf mating hierarchy.

"You should have waited," he said, knowing just how unreasonable that was.

Her eyes grew wide and luminous with the flash of her own anger. "You think I should have stayed some innocent virgin, pining for you forever? You arrogant ass. You said you were never coming home." Her arms straightened, rigid at her sides as she inched towards him. "I do not, for one second, believe you waited a decade for me. How many others were there, Gunner?"

"That's irrelevant," he snapped, his nostrils flared in anger. That was a mistake. With his senses heightened from the wolf lingering so near to surface, the heady scent of her arousal, still clinging to his skin, struck him like a blow. Even though Gunner laid his claim before Pierce's intrusion, his body was primed to mark her all over again and assert his place in her life. Something he doubted she would welcome in her present state of pique.

"I think it is," she said, her voice a feminine growl. "You can't hold me to some idiot double standard. You made it clear ten years ago that you didn't want me for a mate."

Gunner matched her growl with one of his own. Anger mixed with arousal frustrated him but his only means of release were words and he still needed to know where it stood with Pierce. "Regardless of whether you let him, Pierce thinks you're his." Gunner spat out the vile name and pressed on. "He bit you somewhere. Show me?"

Noelle locked eyes with Gunner, her hand drifted to the belt of her robe. She stood rigid for a moment as if she was waging some internal battle. Something flickered in her eyes, not anger but resignation. She pulled the belt and let the robe drop. Somehow, it was not as erotic as it had been before their earlier game of chase. Catching it before it hit the floor, she threw it at him. He let it bounce off his chest and hit the floor.

"Have a good look." Noelle spread her arms and turned slowly.

Gunner drank in the swell of her breasts and the curve of her hip. Her small body was pale and perfect in all but one place, the raw red bite he had placed on her body himself. It would fade to white in time, but Gunner's mark would never leave her body now that he had placed it.

Even knowing she was telling him the truth—Pierce had not marked her and therefore had no claim—there was no stopping the words that tumbled out of his mouth. "You let that filth touch you." Gunner wanted to erase the ghost of Pierce's hands on her body with his own, needed to in the most primal urge he had ever felt.

Gunner moved towards her, his arms reaching out for her. Noelle stepped out of range. She moved with lithe efficiency to put the sofa between them with the dying fire at her back.

"It wasn't one of my finer moments." Noelle said bitterly, her chin raised with pride. She was completely unashamed to be standing there in the buff, as she should be. In Gunner's eyes, she was perfection. "But I'm sure if we looked in your past, there are things you regret."

"Yeah, leaving you." Gunner jammed his bare feet into the abandoned pair of Nikes and headed for the door.

"Where are you going?" Her voice was incredulous.

Gunner knew it looked like he was walking out on her, but if he didn't get some air he was going to explode, and truthfully she should know better. They had a mating pair bond now and he was going to be with her forever. That only left Pierce to be dealt with. Then they could work on why she thought it was possible for him to walk out on her ever. Clouded with the downward edge of his anger and the sexual haze between them, this was not the time to finish this particular chat.

"Clear my head." Gunner pinned Noelle with his stare. "This is not over between us."

Chapter 7

Noelle sat in the corner of the sofa with her knees pulled up to her chest, Gunner's abandoned jacket wrapped around her shoulders. She cradled an empty container of Häagen-Dazs as if the balance of her life hung on its sugary relief. She pressed her face into the upturned collar, inhaling the masculine scent of him, a woodsy aroma that reminded her of nights beside a campfire. *He'll be back*, she reminded herself. He said this wasn't over and she had to trust him, but God was it difficult.

The front door burst open and for a heartbeat Noelle held onto the unreasonable hope that Gunner had come back to continue their honeymoon. Then she looked up and met Laney's wide brown eyes. Noelle jammed another spoonful of ice cream in her mouth to numb herself from the inside out.

"I'm here with supplies!" Laney decreed as she kicked the door closed behind her. She gave Noelle an appraising look and the smile she had been wearing slipped. "Looks like I may not have gotten enough."

Noelle reached out, grasping in the air, and Laney shoved a bottle of dark chocolate syrup in her hand, knowing without words what she wanted. Noelle stripped the plastic off the top, flipped the cap and squirted it directly in her mouth. When she was done, she poured a generous pool of it into her half-full ice cream tub.

Laney shook her head but like any true friend, she made no comment. She abandoned the bottle with Noelle and took the remaining contents of her shopping bag into the kitchen. Noelle heard her friend rattling around in the fridge and speaking low, probably calling Ambrose since the house was as empty as Noelle felt. She hadn't really wanted her brother to know, but the need to stop Laney from telling him didn't outweigh the lethargy that kept her rooted to the sofa.

Staring into the hypnotic lights of her Christmas tree with the spoon dangling from her lips, she contemplated how magical they had seemed when she was lying beneath it with the lights reflected in Gunner's eyes. If she could only just go back to that. But no, her one mistake had to walk in and ruin it all and Gunner had to say those awful things to her.

Noelle hardly took notice when Laney plopped down on the rug, obscuring her view. "First off, blink because—yeah that mile long stare is super creepy. Then tell me what the big jerk said to work you up this much."

She tossed the spoon into the carton and proceeded to fill her friend in on the afternoon's events. "It was both of us really. But if Pierce hadn't come over none of this would have happened," Noelle finished.

"Oh, hon, if you think Pierce wouldn't have been an issue eventually, your problems run deeper then I can handle. We might need a professional."

"Laney, you are a professional."

"Sports psychologist. Not a marriage counselor!"

Noelle tossed a pillow at her friend's head, which she caught and promptly tossed back. In possession of the pillow once again she buried her face in it. "What am I going to do?" she asked, her voice muffled.

"Don't worry. Boys have a way of sorting themselves out." A grin split across Laney's face. "Yeah, I think that's exactly what needs to happen. Don't injure your own cause. Just show up on Christmas day. I'm sure everything will work out fine."

Through Noelle's haze of sugar, she knew she should be worried, but she was too exhausted to puzzle over the cryptic ramblings of her friend. Laney often said strange things when she was puzzling out a problem.

Upgrading the punching bag had been the first thing Gunner did when he took over the decaying building that housed the family business. No more rattling chains when he set the bag in motion with blow after brutal blow. The four foot tall, eighty pound, black vinyl bag hung from straps. All Gunner heard now was the satisfying thud of his fist connecting as the impact rattled through his bones.

Despite his father's pretense of a good show, the old wolf failed epically when it came to actually running his businesses and none had been more neglected than the gym. His mother sold most of the small companies but kept the gym. Gunner knew it was her way of bringing him home. True to form, most of the equipment was top of the line, at least the equipment that the standard yuppie used and the logo, branding, and sign out front were on point. Gunner didn't need a business degree to see that. His father always knew how to keep up appearances, but the building itself had been neglected, membership was down, and it had been years since they were in the black.

After the bags, the mats had been next. The smell of mold and sweat had been too overwhelming to ignore. The new mats were gray. It looked nice after the yellowed walls were freshened with black paint and new mirrors that weren't cracked were added. He bankrolled those renovations expecting he would need them to sell. Now that he knew he was staying, he would splurge on some new weights and maybe a cage for workouts. New memberships had already gone up with his improvements. Who knows what good having a cage might do?

Gunner ignored the tinkle and clink of the silver jingle bells that bounced against the glass of the gym door. Asher closed up to the public over an hour ago. Gunner looked up at the office window that overlooked the gym from the second floor. From behind the glass, his kid brother turned the color of the Santa hat on his head. That meant only one person could be walking through those doors and he was the last person Gunner wanted to be speaking to—well almost.

"You ever thinking about starting a fight team here? Hand pick fighters who share our unique...genetics. Be good to have some new muscle in the pack." The pack leader's tone was deceptively cavalier. Ambrose leaned against the wall facing Gunner, his thumbs hooked casually in the pockets of his worn jeans. His green Henley and puffy orange sport vest looked like they came out of an Eddie Bauer catalogue. He was dressed for a hayrack ride, not the snow falling, laying down a thick wet blanket outside.

"I'm giving up fighting," Gunner said between punches. He focused on the bag, channeling all his pent up rage into a single point.

Ambrose shook his head and frowned. "Damn shame."

"You're not here to talk about my career."

"Ya got me." Ambrose nodded, the corner of his mouth hitched up with that disarming grin. "I got two phone calls you might know something about."

"That so?"

Ambrose moved along the wall until he stood directly in Gunner's line of sight. "First I got a call from your brother because you're beating the piss out of your bag. I imagine he's cowering in the back office."

Perspiration dripped down Gunner's forehead, the salt water stinging his eyes. He blinked it away and returned to the bag, unleashing another vicious combination starting with the left jab, then moving to the left hook and right hand. His whole body moved in accord with his fists, creating a harmony of force.

Ambrose pressed on, unfazed by Gunner's typical silence. "But the call that really got my attention was from Laney."

Gunner turned into a spinning elbow that connected with a load thud; it echoed through the nearly empty gym. "Don't know a Laney." His voice came out a harsh rasp between panting.

"Sure you do. Tall blonde, likes to spike the punch at parties while wearing skin tight, inappropriate t-shirts." The corner of Ambrose's mouth crooked up in a lopsided smile as he described the woman who had embarrassed Gunner thoroughly in the Victoria Secret earlier that day.

"Oh, her. Met her at the mall. Sounds more like your type." Gunner forced his gruff tone to be offhand as he snatched up the towel from the floor where he left it.

Hiding his face in the soft white terry cloth, his mind raced back to Noelle—that robe pooled at her feet and later thrown in his face. Had that episode in her living room been just this afternoon? It felt like, with the early evening's turmoil, Noelle and Gunner had packed at least a couple of the missing years into one day. Gunner knew that was what really brought Ambrose here—his sister. Her brother was just taking his sweet theatrical time getting to the point. Gunner sometimes thought his pack leader missed his true calling as a storyteller.

"Laney called to tell me she talked to my sister and she sounded upset." Ambrose paused for his usual effect. He pushed off the wall and moved forward to steady the bag, his face peering around the edge. When his build-up elicited no discernible reaction from Gunner, he sighed and pressed on. "Noelle told her to show up with eggnog ice cream and the biggest bottle of Special Dark chocolate syrup she could find. Know anything about that?"

Gunner started to walk away but turned at the last second. Still in range, he threw a high kick into the bag that sent his friend stumbling back two steps, but Ambrose somehow managed to maintain his grip. It should have sent him flying. He was their leader for a reason.

"Since you've got intel, did your informant tell you that Pierce Matheson stormed into your sister's house, drunk off his ass?"

Ambrose shrugged and stepped away from the bag, remaining noncommittal. Only the tension around his eyes, leaving a furrow across his brow, gave away just how little he knew about it. "And I'm sure you did me proud and showed him the door."

"I'd have been glad to," Gunner said as he collapsed onto a nearby weight bench, "but your sister shoved me into the bathroom to hide."

Ambrose punched the bag, which sent it swinging as he moved around it, his relaxed demeanor gone as he stalked, pacing back and forth in front of the weight bench. "What the hell did you stay in there for?"

"I didn't. I moved closer to listen and got myself an education. He thinks he's her mate."

"Over my dead body." Ambrose's voice came out a low threatening growl. One thing the pack knew all too well—never mess with their leader's sister. It was one of the reasons Gunner had resisted the temptation she posed for so long.

Gunner had always been viscerally aware of Noelle. As children, he was in awe of her courage. She was small and more fragile than the other pack children, with their rough and tumble nature, but she refused to back down. The first time he witnessed her eyes glow a bright luminous jade after besting one of her bullies, he was smitten. Not that he would have admitted it to Ambrose. Her brother spent all his time punishing the bullies she couldn't deal with on her own, bullies like Pierce.

When Noelle got to high school, he became aware of her on a new level. She had blossomed like one of the hothouse flowers she adored. They had circled each other, two predators testing. A casual touch here and there, long heated looks, and lengthy conversations about the future. But they never crossed the implied boundary of friendship until that night in his car.

Gunner clenched his towel tightly in one hand and sat up straighter, his shoulders back. "The only mark on her is mine and it's gonna stay that way." He met Ambrose's cold eyes—frosty aqua that matched his sister's—and braced for a brutal response from his leader.

Ambrose stopped moving forward as he crossed his arms in front of his chest, his stance wide and loose. He had a way of making himself comfortable anywhere. "Glad to hear it man." The alpha's good-old boy grin returned. "But that doesn't tell me why you're here beating up a bag instead of making my sister happy."

"You're okay with me being with your sister?" Gunner's jaw went slack. When Ambrose's smile spread, Gunner shook his head and closed his gaping mouth.

"Always was. Why the hell do you think I kept telling you about her in my letters and emails? Nobody safer for her. But—" Ambrose punched the air in front of him with his finger, his voice resumed its menacing growl, "you better not make me regret it."

"Too late." Gunner grimaced, looking down and away from Ambrose. "I didn't believe her at first about Pierce, not after the way he acted. We argued about it and I made her prove he hadn't marked her. Told her she should have waited for me."

Ambrose cursed and stepped back from Gunner. Then turned and kicked at the edge of the mat. "You might as well have called her a hussy. You're lucky I don't shred you. You're lucky she didn't."

Gunner rested his elbows on his knees in dejection. His misplaced anger bled away while his hands gripped the towel, twisting it until the scrap of fabric looked the way his gut felt. "I know it's bad. Now how do I fix it?"

"By doing exactly what I tell you to do."

Ambrose could be a sick SOB when he wanted to. Whatever he did, Gunner was sure he wasn't going to like it. But what choice did he really have at this point? "None," he said out loud to himself. Ambrose just nodded as though he knew the question Gunner had answered—the bastard probably did.

Chapter 8

The burden of Noelle's regret dragged at her feet as she went up the ice-slicked driveway to the side kitchen entrance of Ambrose's cabin. Noelle reached up, running her fingers tips over the mark Gunner left, hidden under the collar of her blouse. Every fiber of her being wanted to believe it was going to be all right, but she had one niggling little doubt.

"I should have said yes." Noelle said, as she came to a stop, frozen in front of the door.

An elderly member of the pack brushed past Noelle, jostling the bowl of Jell-O salad she stood clinging to with one arm. The gray-haired matron adjusted her own grip on the Bundt cake she carried and gave Noelle a sidelong glance.

Noelle's mind was stuck on Gunner's proposal and all it meant. In one afternoon—in one moment—he redeemed their broken past. Then her one mistake broke it down again. Her conscience screamed at her and her wolf refused to sleep under the surface. She should have waited for him, but her bigger mistake was shoving Gunner in the bathroom and opening that door. Laney said Ambrose promised Gunner would be here. She would show him everything had changed—she had changed.

Noelle took a deep breath and slipped through the kitchen door. The mingled scents of turkey and ham, with yams and corn casserole assembled for the annual

Christmas potluck, drew her in despite the off-putting buzz of activity. It was a jolting contrast to the quiet of the early winter evening outside, where only her agitated she-wolf preyed on her thoughts. Members of the pack moved through the crowded kitchen with slow cookers and casserole dishes, avoiding near collisions like choreographed dancers.

Her eyes skipped over the familiar faces until it landed on Mrs. Thoren, in her red sweater set and pearls, as she fussed over a tray of deviled eggs. If Gunner was here, as her brother suggested and if his feelings had changed the way she feared, his mother would know about it.

Noelle crossed the kitchen holding up her salad bowl as if it were a shield. "Mrs. Thoren, I know you're busy but can I talk with you for a moment?"

The prim matriarch that held the Thoren family together gave Noelle a critical look. She shook her head with a soft *tsk* as she eyed Noelle from her knee high boots and denim pencil skirt, up to her untamed curls. "I don't have time right now. I need to get this out to the rabid wolves and judging by your appearance, you might want to check a mirror and rethink some things. You look like you've been on a crying jag and you're overcompensating."

Noelle's free hand flew to her mess of curls. She had added extra feathers since Gunner always seemed to notice, but there was nothing wrong with her makeup or her outfit. "I'll take it under advisement. I just have something to ask. It will only take a second." She set her serving dish down and began to unpack it, in hopes her busy hands might keep her rising anxiety in check. "I have to know, if I'm going to make it through tonight."

Mrs. Thoren turned with her hand on her hip. "Out with it then."

"Is Gunner here? Did he tell you about me?"

"Don't you know?" His mother's nose scrunched up as though she was annoyed but returned to her task, adding the deviled eggs to one side of the relish tray.

"If I knew I wouldn't be asking."

"Of course he's here," Mrs. Thoren answered. "You're mated now; he came for you. And you might try looking like you're happy about it instead of like you've been crying out your regret. He's a good man and he deserves a good woman."

Noelle felt the burn under her skin as she lowered her hands to her sides in balled fists, the better to control her claws. "I regret a lot of things. He isn't one of them. I love him."

Gunner's mother blanched at Noelle's words. "He came home so angry and you look like you've been crying for a week. I thought..."

Of course, his mother blamed her. It was always the witch's fault. Didn't matter that her magic wasn't what they all thought it was. She could lay protection and had an extra animal to call; her emotions affected the snow and wind a little. She had never been a danger to anyone. Yet everything was her fault. Even his mother thought he was too good for her.

"Don't worry, I'm fixing this today," Noelle said. "He is a good man and we finally deserve to be happy."

Abandoning her dish, Noelle turned on her heels and marched from the kitchen with her head held high. She made it into the hall before the anger that carried her started to burn away. She raced for the half-bath at the end of the hall. When the door clicked closed behind her she leaned against it and took a deep shuddering breath. Ten minutes and this day was already a disaster. That had to be a record.

Noelle moved to the sink. She stared at her knuckles, quickly turning white like the porcelain she gripped. The last thing she wanted was to meet her own gaze in the mirror. Had she overdone her makeup today? She didn't want to think so a minute ago, but she couldn't face her pack or Gunner with the shadows of her sleepless night or her red-rimmed eyes. Noelle had been on a crying jag, just not for the reason his mother thought. She told his mother she would fix it today, but she wasn't so sure she had it in her, not with the whole pack there to witness the fallout. With one shaking hand, she pulled her phone free of her pocket and fired off a lame text to Laney backing out.

Letting out a slow sigh of relief, the tension bled out of her, until she looked back down at her left hand. She still had on his ring. A harpy from the depth of Tartarus couldn't pry it off her finger. This meekness in her was like poison. She needed to find him and tell him how she felt. She just had to get over herself first.

The soft click of the door drew Noelle's attention. She looked up into the mirror to see Laney standing behind her.

"When I got your text, I figured it was you that was holed up in here. I heard about your run in with Mama Wolf." Laney always did have a way of getting straight to the point. Her dark eyes met Noelle's in the mirror.

"That was fast." Noelle turned to face her friend, leaning her back against the sink.

Laney shrugged and then crossed her arms over the Grinch t-shirt she thought appropriate for Christmas dinner. Bold white letters asked *define naughty*. "I'm not letting you out of this. You can't go on miserable."

"I don't intend to," Noelle conceded. "But I can't do it here. I'm going home."

She made a move for the door but Laney stepped sideways to block her, pursing her lips and looking down her nose at Noelle. "If you're leaving this bathroom, it isn't to go home. You are spending Christmas Eve with your family and friends. Not wallowing in your own misery."

"Don't be like this, Laney."

"I'll *be* however I need to." Laney poked her finger at Noelle's chest to emphasize her point. "I'm sure the last thing you want is for Mama Wolf to think she's right, that you don't really want her son."

"You know about that?"

"The whole pack heard it."

Great. That was just what she needed. They already knew. She thought this day couldn't get any worse. She was wrong.

"Just come out there with me. We'll stick close to your brother and Gunner will find you. It's going to be okay. You'll see."

Laney took Noelle's hand in hers and pasted on the fakest expression of reassurance that Noelle had ever seen, complete with pleading puppy dog eyes.

"Laney, do you know something?"

"What makes you say that?"

Noelle snatched her hand back. "The last time you said something like that I ended up in a crazy awkward situation with Gunner. It almost feels like you're setting me up."

"Would I do such a thing?"

Noelle, stared at the were-bear for a beat, letting her silence answer for her.

When the corner of Laney's mouth quirked up and her eyes filled with wicked mirth, Noelle gave in, her makeup forgotten. "Fine, I can see I'm not going to win this argument. Take me to my brother so I can get tonight over with."

Laney clapped her hands with childish glee. "You won't regret it!"

––––––––––––––––––––––––

Gunner snaked one finger under the edge of the white beard strapped to his face to scratch at the tickle of the synthetic hair. Damn Ambrose.

The Santa getup had to be punishment to atone for his bungling with Noelle rather than being part of some larger plan. His friend and pack leader always did have a twisted sense of vengeance.

"You're all ready to go out there, I see." Asher wore another one of those garish holiday sweaters. This one had a *Star Wars* theme featuring Darth Vader in a Santa hat.

Gunner's hand twitched with the need to slap the grin off the little shit's face, but it was Christmas and their mother was in the kitchen. Instead, Gunner patted the pillow tied around his usually trim waist. "Let's get this over with."

Hoisting the sack of presents, Gunner made his way out to the living room. As he crossed to the chair set up for him, a rabid pack of tiny wolf children swarmed his legs. At least the chair was in the perfect position to maintain his surveillance of the entire room. If she came in and Pierce made a move, Gunner would know even if he couldn't do anything about it.

For the first time he appreciated his pack leader's scheming mind. In this horrendous get-up, Pierce would be less likely to notice him and start a fight be-fore Noelle got there. Even now, the bastard circled the room, a beer in one hand, on the prowl for her. A low growl rumbled through Gunner before he could squash it down.

"Cool it, Santa," Asher warned as he led the first child over. He managed to herd them into a sloppy line. Leaning in, Asher whispered, "Ask 'em if they've been good and hand 'em a present. The sooner we get through this, the sooner you can lose the beard."

Gunner nodded once as the first child scrambled into his lap. She was decked out like a department store holiday ad in her green and red plaid dress and wore a comically large bow in her hair.

"What's your name, little girl?"

The child smiled, revealing a missing front tooth. "My name is Cindy."

Cindy Lou Who popped into his head and he squashed the desire to roll his eyes at the ridiculous direction of his thoughts. "Have you been a good girl, Cindy?"

The girl rattled off some inane answer, but he couldn't hear it over the rush of his own heartbeat when Noelle walked in, dragged behind her crazy friend Laney.

Noelle's posture was stiff and her eyes cast down more like a beta than the alpha he knew she was, trying to escape notice as she made her way to her brother. She was a perfectly packaged present just for him in that little denim skirt and soft white sweater. And the feathers, not hidden like they were before, but worn proudly just for him.

"Santa?"

He looked down at the little person still perched on his knee. Crap—what was he supposed to do next? Asher nudged his shoulder and held out a box, wrapped in shiny green paper and topped with a candy cane. Oh yeah.

He took the box from his brother and handed it to the little girl. "Since you've been so good, Cindy, I have special gift for you. Merry Christmas."

She hugged it to her chest. "Thank you, Santa!"

Cindy dropped to the floor and ran to her parents as Asher lifted the next child up. On and on it went. Children spilled their souls as if he was a jolly old confessional that rewarded with gifts. They didn't seem to notice Gunner's distraction as he tracked Pierce's and Noelle's movements like stars stranded on opposite ends of their orbits. They moved around the room, as far apart as Ambrose could keep them.

Finally, the last kid in line sat balanced on the end of Gunner's knee. The boy droned on about pulling his sister's pigtails and hiding her favorite doll.

Pierce had evidently obtained the threshold of liquid courage he needed and made a beeline to Noelle and her brother. A low growl rolled through Gunner.

"Are you okay, Santa? I didn't mean to be so bad."

Gunner blinked down at the boy's scrunched-up freckled face. "No need to worry, young man. Here, take this present and run along. You made it on the right list this year."

Pierce's voice cut above the ambient noise of the pack milling around them; his hand grasped Noelle's elbow. "When are you going to tell the pack that I'm her mate?"

There was an audible gasp and Gunner tore his gaze from the scene unfolding across the room in time to see his mother. The meddling matchmaker's eyes grew wide when they met her son's before she could retreat behind the false safety of the buffet table with her tray of deviled eggs.

"Maybe we should move this conversation out to the back deck. We're attracting an audience." Ambrose gestured at the sliding glass door behind them with his beer bottle.

Gunner recognized the stubborn press of Noelle's lips as her aggravation grew. If he knew his girl, the pack was about to get a show because she wouldn't back down to any bully—especially not this one.

"He won't make that announcement because I'm not yours to claim." The ring Gunner placed on Noelle's finger flashed like a beacon as she clenched her fist and jerked free of Pierce. "If you have something to say, you can say it to me and not talk over me to my brother."

"I've made my claim…"

"You tried. Don't suppose you'd like the other pack females or for that matter my brother—your pack leader—to know how that turned out for you, would you?" She spat the question at him with thinly-veiled contempt.

Gunner handed the boy to Asher and stood slowly, the chains of his control straining as the wolf within him raged even as her venom bolstered his faith. Her shoving him in the bathroom had triggered him on such a deep level that he had allowed his male pride to take over and only hear Pierce's lies. He had failed her in that moment. Never again.

Ambrose's eyes narrowed dangerously as he swirled the contents of his bottle in a lazy circle. "Pierce, there somethin' you wanna tell me?"

If Pierce wasn't worried about Gunner showing up to kick his ass for pawing on Noelle, he should be worried about the good old boy tone Ambrose had used. Years of friendship told Gunner heads were about to roll if their leader didn't like what he heard.

Those milling around the trio backed away in stunned silence while the rest of the pack continued with their holiday merriment, unaware of the deteriorating scene unfolding under their collective noses.

Pierce ignored the threat their pack leader posed and grabbed Noelle's left hand squeezing it just below the ring. "Where the fuck did you get this?"

Gunner moved without conscious thought, allowing his wolf to take over as he prowled towards his prey. Pierce had messed with the wrong wolf's mate.

Distantly he heard his mother's voice. "Young man, don't you ruin that suit! It costs money."

It was too late; the change flowed over him like water as he moved. The sounds of the party reverberated to a deafening roar as his wolf's soul took control and his senses sharpened. The rancid stink of Pierce's fear assured the wolf that his opponent was a weak mark.

Pierce bolted, changing midstride, and plunged through the plate glass of the patio door, out onto the deck where Noelle and Gunner had danced to Christmas carols. Today there was going to be a different sort of dance.

Chapter 9

"WOW, Santa's a wolf just like us!"

Noelle looked at the freckle-faced boy, still clutching his present from Santa and then down at the heap of shredded red and white fabric, complete with nylon beard. A shower of feathers floated down like downy snowflakes from the pillow that had given Gunner the appearance of Santa's girth. Her mate's black wolf form rushed past her and through the broken patio door. Noelle stood rooted to the floor, looking back between the exuberant child and the broken glass at her feet.

"Didn't you know, kid? His last name is C-L-A-W-S," Asher explained helpfully. "The humans are spelling it wrong."

Laney laughed. "Good one, Asher."

Twisted up in her own thoughts, Noelle had failed to notice Gunner watching her and Ambrose as they made their circuit, greeting members of the pack while carefully staying out of Pierce's path. Caught up in her maneuvering, she somehow missed the one person she had been looking for.

A bit of drifting fluff brushed the tip of Noelle's nose. It twitched in irritation. Then the sneeze caught her in its grip, tearing through her. The violence of it shook her mind loose and she ran after her mate. Vaguely she was aware of her brother close on her heels as she braced her hands on the deck rail and vaulted herself over, landing in the snow below.

Frosted tree branches with icicles like hanging jewels shimmered in the afternoon sunshine as Noelle raced along the trail cut through the snow. It appeared as a white scar furrowed across the glittered landscape. The cold crept up her limbs, dragging at her with each stride. Her denim skirt was not practical for running in ankle deep snow.

This had to stop before someone got hurt. When Laney said that the boys just needed to fight and get it out of their systems, Noelle hadn't taken her seriously. If this was the plan she had been referring to, Laney was going to have a fight of her own on her hands.

A pain-filled howl cut through the stillness of the afternoon air. The fear that lanced through her at that sound had her digging deep for a burst of speed. She could feel her wolf-soul pushing her boundaries, attempting to force a shift. The she-wolf contained within her wanted to go to her mate. Noelle kept a tight rein on her sister soul. If she shifted, there would be no way to reason with them and stop this madness.

But she could get there faster if she flew. In her desperation, she made a tactical error. She wasn't just a wolf—she was a witch. She leapt into the air as white feathers cascaded down her body, enveloping her. She beat her great wings, allowing them to carry her higher and higher to search.

Noelle circled and scanned the ground with sharpened eyes. Unlike in her wolf form there was no owl soul. Noelle had complete control without any of the animal urges she was used to dealing with. When she took this form, her wolf soul completely retreated, so it felt like she was alone in her body, allowing her to concentrate on finding her quarry.

How far could they have run? She prayed that howl

had come from Pierce, a sign that Gunner had caught him. Then she spotted two dark shapes moving in the trees. A massive black wolf she recognized as Gunner circled a smaller gray wolf, Pierce. A trail of red painted the snow wherever Pierce stepped.

Noelle descended, circling closer to the wolves. Gunner's fangs, stained with blood, stood out to her as his determined growl rumbled through the woods around them. Pierce moved slowly, favoring his left flank while snapping and snarling at his stronger opponent like a feral wolf.

She landed at the outer edge to the south of the circle Gunner had created pacing in the snow, as though he were marking himself a ring for the fight. She stepped forward from her owl, shedding the feathers as snow carried away on the wind.

"Gunner don't," she said, her voice shaking with panic. "I'm your mate. Everyone knows that now. You don't have to do this."

The beast containing her lover's soul turned its massive head towards her. Gunner's steady blue eyes looked out at her, listening to her through his wolf. She reached out her left hand to him so that he could see she wore his ring. He stepped towards her, forgetting Pierce for the moment.

Unfortunately, Pierce had not forgotten them. He chose that moment to lunge.

"Behind you, Gunner!" Ambrose shouted as he wrapped his arm around Noelle's middle, hauling her to safety.

Gunner turned in time to block Pierce's jaws from closing on his throat. The two wolves rolled in the snow where she had been standing seconds before. Gunner came out on top, pinning Pierce to the blood-spattered snow. The weaker wolf continued to snap and fight to get up, as though there were still a chance, refusing to submit.

"You have to stop them," she pleaded. "You're their alpha; you can make this stop."

Her brother looked down at her, his eyes sad. "It's for the good of the pack, Noelle. This fight has to happen or Pierce would eat away at us like a cancer. He will submit and leave the pack as an omega or Gunner has the right to end him. It's his right as your mate."

The words shone a spotlight on her own cowardice. If she had not pushed Gunner away, then none of this would have happened. Had she been brave enough— alpha enough—to claim her mate as she should have, as she would have if she had still been that brash sixteen-year-old in the Camaro, they would be happy. Pierce was an idiot, but he didn't deserve to die because of her weakness. She had to be part of this fight, to drive him away. Only Pierce feared no wolf. He feared her witch.

Closing her eyes to the fight, her feathers flowed around her once more, allowing her to slip from Ambrose's firm grasp. Her brother stumbled back. The beat of her wings against the snow silently whipped up the icy powder around her. Her owl form rose, lifting vertically into the air. She circled the bloody snow, looking for an opening.

The wolves, both battered now, had managed to separate. They circled one another like two fighters assessing each other for weakness. The snow grew wilder, isolating the predators locked in conflict with the blizzard force of Noelle's rising power. Her witch-light cast a vivid green from her eyes, painting the blood soaked snow.

Gunner was patient—stalking. Pierce lunged forward,

jaws snapping, only to be driven back by Noelle as she dive-bombed him. Pierce lunged a second time. Noelle dove down, digging her claws into his spine. Her talons tore into his hide until they hit bone. Pierce turned to bite at her, like a dog chasing his tail. She released him and rose up out of danger only to dive again, this time tearing out a piece of flesh before escaping his jaws. Something had to make Pierce's beast give in. If fighting on two fronts didn't overwhelm him into submission, he would die.

Gunner took the opening and leapt forward. His great black jaws closed around the lesser wolf's neck like a vise and slammed him down. Pierce let out a submissive whine and turned his belly up, ears down flat. Gunner stayed locked on, holding down the lesser wolf.

"Enough," Ambrose bellowed, stepping in at last.

Gunner released Pierce and backed away, coming to stand beside his leader in a protective stance, bloodied fangs still bared. Pierce remained down, rolling onto his belly with his head bowed in a show of complete submission.

Noelle's eyes returned to normal as she released her hold on the wind, allowing the snow to settle so that it covered the mark of violence that had gone down.

"Pierce, you will leave pack territory immediately." Ambrose commanded. "After your deception and treatment of my sister, you are not welcome here. Understand I am allowing you to live but if you ever come here again. My sister's mate will tear you apart and I will allow it."

The now defeated omega yipped his agreement and backed away slowly, with his head down and tail between his legs. Ambrose and Gunner stood watching until he cleared the trees.

Noelle dropped to the ground, landing at a run in her human form. Skidding to a stop on her knees, she threw her arms around Gunner's wolf form. A heady mix of relief, fear, and love raged inside of her with the gale force of a storm in the death throes of winter as it raged against the warmth of spring. She sobbed into his black fur until she felt it change into his smooth warm skin and his arms circled her. The rumble of his low voice soothed her even though she couldn't catch the words.

"I never said *yes*," Noelle wailed between hiccupped sobs. "I didn't even realize it until you were gone. I just didn't want him to taint our beautiful day. I wanted to make him go away and I ruined it instead."

"I'm sorry, baby. I was such an idiot," Gunner whispered against her cheek. He pulled back and framed her tear-streaked face with his massive hands. "You didn't ruin anything. I'm a jealous ass. I came home for you and I am never leaving you again."

Looking up into his eyes, Noelle saw the reflection of her own pain. They both had made mistakes, but if they could find each other again—find home in each other's arms—none of it mattered. There was just one thing to straighten out so they could both be happy. She hadn't forgotten what he said before he put that ring on her finger. "You're going to leave for fights. But it's okay because I'll come with you."

"Noelle, I don't need to—"

"You don't need to sacrifice the future you worked so hard building to atone for our past. We have both suffered long enough."

Then Gunner's mouth was on hers, as if he was claiming her all over again, making all the pain disappear. Kissing him felt like she was flying without her wings. Complete and utter abandon—freedom from the gravity dragging down her body and souls.

Male laughter broke the moment. Gunner pulled back his midnight eyes intent on hers. "What do you want, Asher?"

The kid came bounding across the snow, laughing like a deranged hyena as he stopped beside Ambrose. He held a pair of pants in the air like a trophy.

"Here put these on before you embarrass yourself." He tossed Gunner a pair of jeans that landed beside them in the packed snow. "Ma is headin' this way. So unless you want her to see your frozen balls, I'd get to it."

Gunner rested his forehead against Noelle's, his shoulders shook with silent laughter as he absently twirled one of the white feathers twisted into her hair. "Sounds like Mom is looking for round two. You ready?"

Her eyes went wide; she felt her cheeks flaming with shame. "You heard about that?"

"I think the whole pack heard."

"Gunner Francis Thoren!"

"Francis?" Noelle asked, now suppressing her own laughter. "I don't think she came for me. As much as I hate to have you covering your eye candy, I think you better hurry."

Noelle stood and straightened her skirt, brushing the snow off her knees while he dressed. Only in her owl form could her clothes survive not one but two transitions. She felt Gunner's steady presence at her back and after a moment, he wrapped his arms around her protectively even though he stood in the snow in his bare feet, jeans, and nothing else.

Mrs. Thoren pushed between the pack leader and her younger son. She could have gone around them; she just didn't. She stood with her hands on her hips, feet shoulder width apart—the classic pissed-off mother pose.

"Gunner, you get your butt back to the cabin and help clean up the mess you made. We are having a proper dinner to celebrate the holiday and your mating. The whole pack is waiting and I'll be damned if I am cleaning up that mess."

Noelle tried unsuccessfully to suppress a burble of laughter. She looked up at Gunner as he answered, "Yes, ma'am."

"What are you snickering at, young lady? You're not getting out of this. You can get yourself up here and clean too," Mrs. Thoren complained, her brow pinching together in a scowl.

Noelle schooled her expression into something more contrite as she pushed down the giggles that threatened to bubble back up. "I'm just happy, ma'am. We'll be right there."

"I should hope so." Her new mother-in-law started to march off. She made it ten feet when she stopped and turned back to face Noelle and Gunner. "Welcome to the family, dear."

His mother continued her march back to the house. Ambrose turned to follow, clapping Asher on the back and shoving the kid ahead of him.

Gunner turned Noelle in his arms to face him. Noelle reached up, stroking his dark beard with one hand as she stroked his bare chest with the other. A contented smile cracked his tough exterior.

"What are you so happy about, mister?" Noelle asked.

His eyes seemed to sparkle with laughter. "Baby, I've never been so happy to be home for the holidays."

Gunner pulled Noelle into a souls-searing kiss. She could only agree. This was the best Christmas present she could have wished for.

Epilogue

Noelle's knee bounced in time with her anxiety as she sat in the arena waiting for the next fight—Gunner's title fight. Sitting beneath the glare of hot lights with her unborn child using her bladder as a punching bag, she struggled to contain her wolf soul.

Her heightened shifter sense of smell, exacerbated by what her friends referred to as the pregnancy super sniffer, wasn't helping matters. Every time someone walked past her with beer and food in hand, or reeking of aftershave or pungent cologne, she wanted to hurl all over their shoes. Or steal their hotdog. Pregnancy was a crazy beast but she was determined to enjoy this fight.

This was far from her first time watching her mate and now husband fight live. But cage-side for the championship—yeah, intense didn't cover the range of emotions coursing though her. Pride and anxiety were at each other's throats and she was their battleground.

"Down girl." Laney put her hand on Noelle's knee, forcing her to be still. "Chill-ax. He hasn't even done the walk out yet."

"I can't help it, Laney. I pushed him to do this."

"Can you imagine how intolerable he would be if you hadn't?"

She could actually. She absently rubbed her protruding belly. With their first baby on the way, Gunner had been obsessed with her every move. He took her damn chocolate! They were having a baby not a puppy. Kicking him out of the cabin to go train at the gym had been the only thing giving her peace. Well that—and ice cream.

"I just couldn't let him retire. He worked hard to earn this title fight. I could never forgive myself if he gave it all up for me." She shifted in her seat, rubbing her thighs together. "Besides it's a huge turn on to watch him fight."

"Oh. My. God." Laney's hands clapped together in excitement. "You are totally going to do him in the locker room when this is over, aren't you?"

Heat flooded Noelle's cheeks. "Maybe."

In fact, she had been day dreaming about that very fantasy off and on since the plane landed in Vegas. Of course, Gunner had to win first and no one had beaten Cezar Silva for his last eleven consecutive fights.

The lights dimmed and in direct opposition, Noelle's adrenaline spiked. This was it. Gunner's name surrounded by blue lightning scrolled across the jumbo-tron on a continuous loop as Metallica's *Of Wolf And Man* blasted through the packed arena.

Laney roared with laughter. "I can't believe it! He does have a sense of humor!"

Ignoring her friend, Noelle stood, craning to see Gunner come out from the tunnel where every other fighter that night had emerged. A roar went through the crowd before she spotted him, head nodding to the beat, his eyes cast down in concentration as he strode confidently to the cage with his entourage of trainers following him. He stopped in front of the cutman and a referee. Gunner dragged his shirt over his head and shucked his shoes and socks. His trainers took them away and Gunner turned towards the cutman and the official, arms spread wide for their inspection. After they applied

Vaseline to his eyebrows, he prowled up the stairs as if his inner predator had control rather than the other way around. The image persisted as he made his way to his side of the cage, where he paced with seemingly restless agitation. Gunner rolled his neck and pounded his gloved fists together while he waited for his opponent.

He didn't wait long before the lights dropped again. This time red lights bathed the crowd and Cezar Silva's name scrolled overhead in flashing gold. A Latin pop song replaced the thundering rock anthem, and the crowd once again surged with excitement—this time for the champion. The crowd chanted his name as he emerged from the tunnel with his head down, acknowledging no one.

The man's eyes were dark and hooded with thick scar tissue across his brow. Unlike Gunner, this man wore the mileage of his fights across his face. Even Silva's ears were swollen to near bursting with the ugly cauliflower ear that so many of the fighters had. His shorn scalp did nothing to disguise them. He rolled his shoulders as he walked. They were heavily tattooed with a cross and angel wings, as if he considered himself some kind of pious warrior.

Silva went through the same process to enter the cage. He did not pace. Instead he looked down at the ground, his razor sharp focus evidently turned inward. His body language read fear—not aggression. Noelle had wondered about that when she watched Silva's fight tapes with Gunner. He started every fight this way. If it was fear, he keep it under a tight grip because it never showed once the cage door closed and the fists began to fly.

"Ladies and gentlemen," The announcer bellowed, getting the attention of the rabid fans. "This fight is scheduled for five, five-minute rounds for the Middleweight Extreme Cage Fighting Championship of the World!"

The announcer dramatically turned, pointing his cue cards at Noelle's mate. "Now introducing the blue corner, the challenger: a wrestler and dirty boxer with a professional record of twenty-eight wins, four losses, and one no contest. Fighting out of Ushers Run, Iowa, Gunner 'The Mauler' Thoren!"

Noelle cheered, raising her arms high in the air. The crowd echoed her excitement. In acknowledgement, Gunner pumped his fists overhead and then continued to prowl along the edge of the cage.

Taking control of the crowd once more, the announcer pointed at the champion, his voice pitched for urgency. "And fighting out of the red corner, a Ju-Jitsu fighter with nineteen professional victories, one loss, fighting out of Jacksonville Florida, by way of São Paulo, Brazil..." the announced paused, drawing the moment out, "the reigning, defending, undisputed ECF Middleweight Champion of the World...Cezar 'The Dictator' Silva!"

If she thought the crowd had lost it for her mate, she was wrong. The stadium seemed to vibrate with the energy of their screams and that stupid chant in Portuguese started, "*Uh, Vai Morror!*" Over and over again.

"What the hell is that?" Laney asked covering her ears.

"They're taunting my mate," Noelle answered, her tone clipped. "They're saying, 'You're gonna die.'"

"Let's fight!" The ref barked, serving as the opening bell that shifted Gunner and his opponent both into action.

Gunner raised his fists in front of his chest as they rushed at each other. Silva connected with an overhand right, sending Gunner down on one knee. But Gunner didn't get to challenge for the title by going down that easy. He shot back to his feet when Silva rushed in for a takedown. The Champion lifted Gunner from around the waist and slammed him down on his back. They scrambled for position, each man holding on as they rolled in a bid for control.

Silva's arm snaked around Gunner's neck. He pressed his chin to his chest. The champ hammered the side of Gunner's head baiting him to lift his chin. Gunner knew better. He threw up punches of his own to loosen his opponent's grip.

This was a bad start. He knew it. His coach would be screaming it. But his gas tank would hold up when it counted. Tonight it was going to count. As long as he could keep his chin tucked, he was content to let the fucker burn out his arms. Gunner trained for a five round fight.

Gunner felt his opponent's vice grip loosen. He took the opening to shift his hips and roll. Silva hung on, fighting to roll with it and maintain back control. Gunner pivoted and exploded up, shedding his opponent like water. Silva surged to his feet and Gunner turned in time to catch Silva with a quick jab.

They circled each other, pacing the cage, measuring for weakness. The champ rushed in again, swinging hard and missing. Gunner made him pay for it with two quick jabs. The next rush, his opponent played it safe and came in low for another takedown. Gunner was ready for it and sprawled.

Just keep wearing yourself out, Silva.

The champ went in for another flurry as Gunner heard

the blocks, warning the round was coming to an end. He weathered the storm. Silva could have this round. One was nothing if Gunner took the other four or better yet— finished it out right. The signal for the end of the round came and the ref threw himself between the two men, shoving them apart.

Gunner moved to his corner, dropping onto the waiting stool as he took out his mouthpiece. "Water," he ordered.

"Small sips." His coach pulled the cap and passed it to Gunner. "Alright, Gunner. That's the best he's got. Now we've seen it and we know you got better. So stop holding back and give it to him."

"Those damn takedowns."

"You know how to defend 'em. And if you knock his ass out like you should, they won't matter. Combinations. Start throwin' 'em. Don't throw one punch, throw two. Three'd be better. Overwhelm him. He won't be ready for it 'cause he's lookin' to take you down."

The clap of the blocks carried over the screaming throng, calling the fighters back. Gunner stood, put his mouthpiece back in and slammed his fists together. He glanced to the side and saw his wife, hands cupped to her mouth screaming his name. There was something about seeing his woman—his mate, round with his child and cheering him on that revved him up. Oh yeah—he was walking out of this cage with a belt tonight.

The cornermen cleared out and the cage doors closed once more. Gunner's focus zeroed in on Silva. He rolled his shoulders to stay loose and rocked from one foot to the other—no bounce in his movement. The ref stood in the center of the cage, waiting to give the signal to start. The beast inside Gunner, wolf twin to his human soul, calmed, content with the battle about to begin again.

In the cage, it was vital he stay in absolute control of his other side, but it had never been an issue. They called him "The Mauler" because of his vicious and relentless attacks. His coach, the only shifter trainer hidden in the league ranks, remarked once that it was as if the wolf fought instead of the man. The truth was, in the thick of battle, his souls were in perfect harmony. His wolf receded, completely content to watch the mayhem unfold through Gunner's human eyes. The wolf that the human world had no idea lay hidden within, had nothing to do with the ferocity dealt out by the man.

"Fight!"

Plodding forward, the relentless pace of the first round now appeared to drag at Silva's flat feet. Gunner charged in. He controlled the center this time, forcing his opponent to keep his back to the cage. Silva swung with his right, a power punch that now packed none of the sting it had before. Gunner grinned around his mouthpiece as he bit down and leapt. His knee came up. The impact of his knee striking Silva's jaw radiated up Gunner's leg.

Silva's eyes rolled back. He crumpled against the cage and then the mat, a marionette whose strings suddenly dropped. To ensure that Silva wouldn't recover, Gunner rushed in dropped his fist like a hammer on Silva's unprotected face repeatedly until the ref grabbed him by the waist and hauled him off. It was over.

The cold feeling of peace fell away and Gunner's wolf surged forward in shared excitement. A primal yell tore from his human throat, releasing that energy as he raced to the other side of the cage. He jumped, straddling the padded top of the cage wall, pounding his chest like a mad man. He pointed out at Noelle. Laney was already dragging his mate from her seat towards the cage door. A wide smile graced Noelle's tear-streaked face. She had been by Gunner's side, whether he knew it or not, for most of their lives. She forced him to take this last step. It was her victory as surely as it was his—as it should be between mated pairs.

Coach pulled him down, dragged Gunner through the chaos of officials, to the center of the cage where the ref and announcer waited with the president of the ECF, Darren Black. The ref gripped Gunner's glove raising it up overhead as the announcer made the final call. "Winner by TKO *and NEW* undisputed ECF Middleweight Champion of the World! Gunner"The Mauler" Thoren!"

The ring was a chaotic mess of people: officials, the league president, trainers and doctors fussing over the now former champion. Noelle found Gunner and blinked away the swell of tears that blurred the sight of the ECF belt strapped around Gunner's waist—something she never doubted would happen. Her mate was born for this and for her. He was a warrior in a society where athletes replaced the gladiators that history once venerated in the colosseums.

The first round had been hard to watch, but her faith never wavered. Watching her mate in that second round, his dominance heated her blood. Hell—she turned into a quivering mass of tears and need.

He reached out for her, pulling her snug into his side as he spoke to the commentator interviewing him. As sensitive as her nose was she should have been disgusted by the smell of sweat pouring off him, but instead it ramped her up more. Virile man and leather, the scent made her knees wobble. She bit down on her lip as she pressed her thighs together and burrowed further into her mate's side.

The bald, metrosexual looking guy, with his mani-cured nails and crisp black dress shirt, pressed a mi-crophone in front of her mate's face. Gunner's mouth was moving—answering. Caught in the moment, Noelle watched the joy play across his rugged features, miss-ing the words at first. "And I'd like to thank my wife. I wouldn't be here for any of this without her."

Pride welled up inside of her, bringing with it a new tide of tears. It was official. Noelle blamed the hor-mones. She never cried this much before he knocked her up under the Christmas tree six months ago. That had been the real gift from the holiday. It hadn't been the shedding of their past, but the bright new future they discovered weeks later.

"What's next Gunner? Where do you go from here?"

A half smile lifted the corner of Gunner's mouth. "I'll fight whoever they give me, but I'm moving home to train. I'm starting a family. Building my own team." Gunner's voice raised to a shout. "I'm putting everyone on notice. If you're animal enough to train with"The Mauler," then this is an open invitation!"

"You heard it here first, folks..." the commentator's voice receded.

Gunner turned and dropped to his knees before Noelle, hugging her to him as if she were made of glass. The lights, the cameras, the screaming fans, it all seemed to slide away. Some part of her registered its continued existence. But with him like this, the world narrowed down to the two of them—to this moment. He laid gen-tle a kiss on her round belly. A soft thump, like a finger poking her flesh but from the inside, answered him.

"Thank you," Gunner said, his voice sounding almost choked.

"For what? You did it. I always knew you would."

"For everything. For waiting in that Camaro. For for-giving me. For the feathers in your hair." He shook his head and laid another kiss on her stomach. "For every-thing you give me. *We* did it, baby."

Noelle's heart raced with wicked anticipation as she tugged on his hand, urging him to his feet. Her lips curled into a playful smile as he complied. "Well in that case, I think you better show me the locker room."

About the Author

Cassie Leigh specializes in all things paranormal romance. She has been dreaming up stories since before she could write. It started with recording conversations for her dolls on a Fisher-Price tape recorder, moved on to an antique typewriter found at a garage sale, then an electric typewriter, and finally computers. In all that time, she never thought of herself as a writer. It was only a dream. It wasn't until she picked up romance novels in her late twenties that she started to believe it was more than that and she had found where she belonged. With the help of her husband, she carves out time to write while raising five children, working full time and obsessing over her midcentury modern dream home.

Her goal as a writer is to transform the trials and tribulations of everyday life and turn it on its head using the paranormal world of spirits, vampires, and were-animals. The world can be a scary place, but she finds it a little more tolerable knowing that the supernatural things that go bump in the night have problems just like the rest of us. Want more? You can connect with Cassie Leigh online.

https://www.facebook.com/cassieleighauthor

https://www.twitter.com/cassieleigh322

https://www.amazon.com/author/leighcassie

https://www.cassieleighauthor.com

To get the inside track on all new releases, sign up for her newsletter at

https://tinyletter.com/cassieleigh322

Until Death Do Us Part

Do you like a good ghost story with your romance? Check out the haunted romance series by Cassie Leigh!

Until Death Do Us Part.

Available now from Broken Typewriter Press

The veil between life and death will part to bring two souls together...

Millie was a lonely spirit with no one but her house to keep her company. That changed the day the handsome new owner of her precious home moved in and said hello. She never thought she would have a chance to fall in love again. Now she is chipping away at her past and turning away from the light she thought she was waiting for. There is just one problem; the love of her afterlife is engaged.

Noah and his fiancée are having trouble sharing a vision for a home to grow their future in. Lucky for him the spirit in residence is on his side. Unlike his fiancée, Millie seems to like the changes and an unlikely connection is kindled. Now he is holding out on the hope that their bond will not burn out before their unlikely romance can ignite.

Millie spied the real-estate agent through the rosette window of the attic. She loathed the balding relic that now lumbered up the sidewalk since the day he brought developers to tear down her home. Reason told her she should welcome that fool. He could be bringing potential company into her life. She turned away from the window where she sat perched day in and day out. It made her ache with sadness to see the proud farmhouse that she spent her youth in sit empty, no furniture or voices filling it up. But her feelings were not enough to make her welcome the agent.

Twin metallic clunks from outside broke through the stillness of the morning and sent a fluttering sensation running through Millie's midsection. She paced the dusty pine planks; the prospect of new life carried her nearer the door on each pass. She didn't need to look. It would be better if she kept her distance up here in the attic. Unexplained cold spots and footsteps that had no apparent source tended to scare people away.

When the jingle of keys and muffled voices echoed up the stairs, her curiosity won out. Surely she could get a glimpse of them from the stairs. There was no need to go down.

The front door closed with a thud that reverberated through Millie.

The droning voice of the real-estate agent assaulted her ears. "It's a fixer upper but the neighborhood is quiet and it's in one of the better school systems."

Millie rushed to the landing and leaned over the carved wooden banister. "Don't you mess this up," she shouted down at the agent, whose heavy footsteps she heard lurking in the front room. "Tell these people what a lovely home this was. I'm sick to the teeth of being alone."

Millie blew out a long breath, a habit that was no longer necessary. Why did she bother, the real-estate agent couldn't hear her. She rubbed her hands along the polished rail. It couldn't hurt to go down and take a peek at who the inept fool brought this time. Millie shifted back and forth on the balls of her feet, unable to hold still. No, they'll come to her. She just needed patience—a commodity she had precious little of, unlike time.

"The more we see, the better I like this house." A man's clear baritone echoed off the bare walls of the kitchen in tandem with the banging of cabinet doors. Millie supposed the man behind it was going through opening and closing them as he considered his purchase.

The potential buyer walked into the entryway, leading

a woman by the hand towards the stairs where Millie sat. To the diminutive Millie, he seemed tall and dark. When he glanced up the stairs, sharp blue eyes met her own. Even from this distance, Millie felt captive to the vitality that filled them. Though she knew better, she felt as if there was something in that look just for her, some message she wasn't grasping.

He looked away, back at the woman he came with. The absence of his gaze broke whatever unlikely cord of communion had been strung between him and Millie. He couldn't have seen her, no one ever did. Millie's cheeks tingled, remarkably like blushing, if that had been possible. She raised a hand to her cold cheek. He certainly was the best-looking man that the portly agent had ever brought through her home and closer to Millie's age than most of them.

"Noah, I really don't want something that needs this much work," said the man's companion. "I just wanted to walk in after the wedding to our picture perfect starter home." The woman's blonde ponytail swayed as she shook her head.

The woman wore a modern, soft pink sweater that came down to mid-thigh of her form-fitting denim. Millie looked down at her own shapeless ivory dress. It hung past her white stocking-clad knees. Perhaps Millie could have had a better husband if she had been as attractive.

Noah started up the stairs, hand in hand with his future wife. They must have money, Millie assumed, because he appeared as richly dressed as the pretty blonde, with her collared shirt and pullover sweater. Her working-class husband and father would have called him a well-to-do lawyer's son, or maybe a banker. Definitely not the kind of man Millie was used to being around.

Mindful not to touch the couple as they passed her, Millie scooted out of the way. She made no effort to conceal herself further. The woman looked past Millie into the bathroom, appearing completely unaware of her presence. Noah looked right at Millie. She gasped and then ducked behind an open bedroom door, kneeling down. Her heart racing, she peered through the gap below the hinge. When Noah continued into the first bedroom without comment, Millie sighed in relief and moved back into the hall.

He must have been looking though her. It was silly on her part to continue deluding herself that he could actually see her. Just an over-active imagination brought on by decades of loneliness, she chided herself. Only children ever noticed her and usually only the very young. She took extra care not to frighten the little darlings.

"What do you think of this one for the master, Claire?" Noah asked.

"The closet is so small and the carpet has to go. It'll kill my allergies and my asthma will flare up," she whined in reply. Her cheeks sucked in and her mouth pursed in a pretty pout.

"I can fix that," Noah promised. He began to count off the benefits on strong hands that appeared rough and used to work, much to Millie's surprise. "Just think of the possibilities. This house is under budget and we were only looking for three bedrooms; this house has four. The room adjoining this one could be turned into a master bath and walk in closet."

His plan sounded lovely to Millie. Someone to care for her home and remake it into a special place again, like it had been before her life had fallen apart.

"I don't want to live in a construction zone." Claire

crossed her arms in front of her chest and took a step back. "I want move-in ready."

Millie's jaw dropped and she drifted up beside Claire. "Be reasonable, not every man offers to do something so monumental, you silly woman. Don't you see how lucky you are?" Millie asked, waving her hands in agitation.

"You'll have that." Noah reached out, resting his hand on Claire's arm. "We have three month's until the wedding. All I need is eight weeks."

"I'm listening." Claire looked away, as if only humoring him.

He moved in close, his voice lowered to a whisper. "I'll move in and start working. You stay in your place and focus on the wedding. You'll move in when we get back from Hawaii."

Mille held her breath, her hands tented together and covering her mouth as she drifted backwards into the hall. Was it too much to hope that this seemingly ungrateful woman would accept such a generous offer from her betrothed?

Claire sighed and her arms dropped to her sides. "Well, I'll get to pick my own finishes. I couldn't do that in a house that's already done, there's that at least."

Millie clapped in excitement and spun happily. Finally, some company.

Noah grinned and grabbed for Claire's hand. "I knew you'd see. Let's talk to Bob and put in our offer."

Millie beamed with hope from her spot in the hallway. Noah pulled Claire behind him, striding with purpose to the stairs. Millie stepped back out of the way until her waist pressed against the handrail. Noah returned Millie's smile with genuine warmth and a slight nod, silently offering a hello. He didn't pause as he continued down the stairs, leaving Millie disoriented. Her own smile slipped away. Did he see her after all?

Follow You Anywhere

when strange events begin to emerge, Bettina is convinced something followed her home.

Seth Hynek accepts the solitude of his afterlife. Brooding and reliving the hellish memories of World War II are more tolerable when he's alone. But something changes when he sets out to scare off the group of women who've invaded his home. One of the women sparks something in him—something he can't identify. Keen to know more about Bettina, he follows her home, realizing he can communicate with her through her dreams. But when Bettina's ex-husband finds her and threatens her, Seth fears he can't protect her. Once again, Seth is haunted by the idea that he can't save the one woman who needs him the most. With their pasts colliding with the present, will their ghostly romance end before they can find a way to create a future together?

———————————————

Bettina stared out the car window, up at the imposing Victorian mansion with the moon rising behind it. Someone had made the unfortunate mistake of painting it black. It looked like something out a children's Halloween storybook. Shutters hung at haphazard angles, waiting for a strong wind to catch hold and send them flying. The idea of walking across the compromised structure of the slumped porch made her blood run cold, but her friends Amanda and Charity were testing her new resolve not to live in fear, and she would see it through.

As the new girl in Glennbluffs, a small tourist town on the Mississippi side of Iowa, she was happy to have made friends so easily and she didn't want to let them down. She hoped this was going to be the first of many new experiences for her. In California, fun on a Friday night never included a ghost hunt unless you were watching it on TV.

Charity knocked on the glass. "Bettina, get your skinny ass out of the car."

Despite the fact they were all on a collision course with their thirties, Bettina's friend looked like a pinup, roller-derby chick with a thing for Rainbow Brite. For to-day's ensemble, she had dyed her hair electric blue and tied it up with a red bandana that matched her cherry bomb lipstick, *à la* Rosie the Riveter. Charity dressed as though unconcerned with the nip in the air that came with autumn. The sleeves of her chambray button-down were rolled up and she had belted her denim shorts with a skinny red belt. She finished the look with high-heeled tennis shoes that looked like crayons threw up.

As ordered, Bettina got out of the car. Her colorful friend pranced over to the van parked ahead of her own silver Prius.

Charity reminded Bettina of home, which is probably why Bettina had gravitated to her for friendship and the reason Bettina put up with her crass way of ordering her around. Outsiders in a small town stuck together.

Amanda poked her dark head out from between open doors at the back of her van. Bettina's conservative friend stood out with her stark devotion to wearing all black and her severely layered hairstyle. Amanda was a local—or had been. She didn't have to be an outsider. But she'd gone to the big city for beauty school and came back to her town with a decidedly modern attitude that many of the old timers resented. She hadn't told Bettina why she'd come back but that was okay. Bettina hadn't shared that she was hiding from her ex-husband.

"Glad you're here," Amanda said. "You can help me with some of this stuff."

Amanda hopped down from the back, then lugged out two black cases on rollers. She shoved the largest case towards Charity before taking up a massive coiled extension cord that ran back to something inside the van.

"What's this all for?" Bettina asked as she scurried over to help.

She grabbed the remaining rectangular hard case and began pushing it up the sidewalk towards the house. With each step, she resisted the urge to scan every bush or tree up and down the street for danger. There was safety in numbers.

"Computer monitors, video cameras, hand held audio recorder...."

Bettina cut Amanda off. "Do we really need all of this?"

"Duh."

"Of course." The two women answered over each other.

Charity used her box on wheels like a surfboard, shoving off with one foot and balancing her stomach on top as she glided past Amanda and Bettina. The front wheels hit the bottom wooden step, sending Charity lurching forward. She planted her feet on the ground and grabbed the edge of the box to keep from falling off.

"Stop clowning. It's time to get some work done," Amanda grumbled as she marched up the wood stairs. Each board groaned in protest as she went.

Bettina stared warily at the steps, watching intently as Charity lumbered up dragging her box after her. If rickety wood planks could stand her friends' abuse, they could stand her meager weight. Gingerly she placed one foot on the step and then another. When the board held, she dared herself to try the next step and then the next until she found herself next to her friends at the top.

Charity's eyebrow rose in question. "Afraid the steps are gonna bite you?"

Bettina shrugged. "More like cave in."

"Come on," Amanda said. She had unclipped a large ring of keys from the handle of Charity's equipment case and used them to open the door. "We need to get set up."

Amanda walked inside, trailing the cord after her without waiting to see if they would follow. Charity winked and went in, leaving Bettina standing there alone. Bettina couldn't bring herself to go into the darkness beyond the door as her friends so easily did. She shifted her weight back and forth, causing the porch to let out an ominous moan like a distressed whale. It was incentive enough to propel her feet through the door, dragging the rolling case after her.

"Amanda? Charity?" Consumed in her own fear, she hadn't watched which direction they'd gone. From the corner of her eye, Bettina caught a glimpse of movement on her right. She turned to find a carved wooden banister and wide staircase looming before her, illuminated by the moonlight through the open door as if this path had been marked just for her.

There was a tap on Bettina's shoulder.

"What are you looking at?" Amanda asked.

Bettina whipped around and lost her balance in the process. She steadied herself on the rolling case. "It was nothing. Just thought I saw something."

"Don't be so antsy. You're probably not going to see much until we review our footage later. Come help us get set up in the dining room." Amanda held out a flashlight, which Bettina took gladly and then took over Bettina's case, leading her away from the stairs.

They passed through what Bettina assumed might have been either the living room or the formal parlor. Floral wallpaper hung on the walls, partially scraped off in places and in others hanging in limp sheets as though the glue had given up the ghost. Heavy velvet drapes sagged, blocking out the ambient streetlight. Furniture sat stacked back in a corner, covered with a sheet that had yellowed with age.

The second parlor had a different color palette than the first, or so it seemed in the dim glow of the little light she carried. In the darkness, it was difficult to tell. It might have been the lack of dust-covered furniture or the atmosphere itself that gave the perception.

In the dining room, a rickety folding table had been set up or left behind by someone. A single portable work lamp stood sentinel over it, shining down on the equipment Charity had already made a dent in un-packing. Equipment she had no name for, along with the promised cameras and tape recorders, littered the makeshift station. She couldn't imagine what was left in this last smaller case. Amanda flipped it up onto the table and pulled out three flashlights and the largest lap-top Bettina had ever seen.

"What is that for?" Bettina asked.

Flipping the monstrosity open, Amanda didn't look up as she started the process of logging in. "I brought it in case there was any footage we want to check right away. If you think you hear something or see something we can download it and watch it on the full screen."

They seemed to take this so seriously. Bettina consid-ered the money they must have invested in equipment and then her gaze landed on the power cord that led back outside to the van. Dang, they even had their own generator. Bettina reached up, twisted her hair into a ponytail in a nervous gesture, and then released it as she rocked from one foot to the other, suppressing the urge to flee. This was just a lark, she told herself—at least it was for her. They wouldn't find anything. She didn't believe in this sort of thing. That's why it was safe to come out with the girls. It was a harmless adventure.

Amanda looked up at her from the laptop, her eyes narrowed. "You remember what we talked about right? You gonna make it?"

Bettina nodded, but she felt the heat rise in her cheeks. "No freaking out. It corrupts the evidence. I can hold it together. I promise."

Already lost in her work, Amanda nodded her acceptance of the answer.

Bettina had spoken honestly. She could hold her tongue, had done so before in more dire circumstances. Certainly a little fright wouldn't make her scream, but her friends didn't know that about her, and she was keen to keep it that way.

Coming Soon

Need another Haunted Romance?
Good news, there is one more to come…

Coming in 2017 from Broken Typewriter Press

www.ingramcontent.com/pod-product-compliance
Lightning Source LLC
Chambersburg PA
CBHW062023190726
48284CB00014B/2636